William Powell Frith, John Leech

John Leech

Vol. 1

William Powell Frith, John Leech

John Leech
Vol. 1

ISBN/EAN: 9783337400514

Printed in Europe, USA, Canada, Australia, Japan

Cover: Foto ©Raphael Reischuk / pixelio.de

More available books at **www.hansebooks.com**

JOHN LEECH

His Life and Work

BY

WILLIAM POWELL FRITH, R.A.

WITH PORTRAIT AND NUMEROUS ILLUSTRATIONS

IN TWO VOLUMES
VOL. I.

LONDON
RICHARD BENTLEY AND SON
Publishers in Ordinary to Her Majesty the Queen
1891

I Dedicate this Book

TO

CHARLES F. ADAMS,

LEECH'S EARLIEST, WARMEST, AND MOST CONSTANT FRIEND;

WITH MY GRATEFUL THANKS

FOR THE INTEREST HE HAS TAKEN IN MY WORK,

AND FOR THE VALUABLE ASSISTANCE AFFORDED

IN THE EXECUTION OF IT.

PREFACE

I AM very conscious of the many sins of commission and omission of which I have been guilty in my attempt to write the "Life and Work of John Leech"; but, that ingratitude may not figure amongst my shortcomings, I take advantage of the usual preface to acknowledge my obligations to friends and strangers from whom I have received assistance, and to express my warmest thanks for their kindness.

The time that has elapsed since Leech's death has terribly thinned the ranks of his friends and contemporaries; but the leveller has spared and dealt tenderly with one of his earliest and most constant friends, Mr. Charles F. Adams, whose store of Leech's letters, together with many pleasing reminiscences, have been placed unreservedly at my disposal. From Mr. Kitton's memoir of Leech I have derived, through the author's kindness, much advantage; and to Mr. Thornber, a well-known collector of Leech's works, I owe the opportunity of selecting some of the best illustrations that grace the book.

I also desire to express my gratitude to the proprietors of *Punch*, who, though unable to comply with my unreasonable demand to the full extent of it, have given me most important help in my endeavours to do honour to the genius who was such an honour to *Punch*. I owe to those gentlemen no less than eight of the full-page illustrations, to say nothing of numbers of small cuts.

I take this opportunity of thanking Mr. Grego, my neighbour Mr. McKenzie, Mr. Willert Beale, and Mr. Maitland for their help in various ways; not forgetting the Eton boy, whose anonymity I preserve according to his desire.

To Sir John Millais, Mr. Ashby Sterry, Mr. Horsley, Mr. Holman Hunt, and Mr. Cholmondeley Pennel I also offer my warmest acknowledgment for the papers they have so kindly contributed.

In conclusion, I permit myself a few words in explanation of that which I know will be laid to my charge, namely, that my book tells too little of Leech and too much of his work, and that it is chronologically deficient. In excuse I plead that the life of Leech as I knew it from its early days was, like that of most artists, entirely devoid of such incidents as would interest the public; and that from the difficulty of acquiring certain information, and the varying times at which it was supplied, chronological accuracy was impossible.

CONTENTS OF VOL. I.

LIST OF ILLUSTRATIONS

———◦◦◦———

JOHN LEECH:

HIS LIFE AND WORK

———

PROLOGUE.

"'*LEECH*' (*spelt '* leich*') is an old Saxon word for* '*surgeon,*'" *writes a friend to me.* "*Hence, as you know, the employment of the word '* leech*' as a term applied in former times to doctors.*"

Though Leech is not a common name, I have met with several bearers of it under every variety of spelling that the word was capable of—Leech, Lietch, Leich, Leeche, Leitch, etc. Only two of the owners of these names became known to fame—John, of immortal memory, and, longo intervallo, William Leitch, a Scottish artist, and landscape-painter of considerable merit, whose pictures, generally of a classic character, found favour amongst a certain class of buyers. A large subject of much beauty was engraved, and, I think, formed the prize-engraving for the year for the Art Union of London. I have no doubt William Leitch was frequently asked if he were related to John. The sound of the names was similar, and few inquirers knew of the difference in

*the spelling.   Whether William was asked the ques-
tion or not I cannot speak to with certainty; but that
John was I am sure, because he told me so himself,
and, as well as I can recall them, in the following
words:*

*"I was asked the other day if I were related to a
man of the same name—a Scotchman—a landscape-
painter.   He spells his name L-e-i-t-c-h, you know.
I said, 'No; the Scotch gentleman's name is spelt in
the Scotch way, with the 'itch in it.'   Not bad, eh?
I hope nobody will tell him!"*

*I met William Leitch several times (he died long
ago), and was always charmed by his refined and
gentle manner; but we never became intimate, so I
cannot say I had the following anecdote from himself;
but it was told me by an intimate friend of the artist,
who assured me that he had it from Leitch direct.*

*Leitch had a considerable practice as a drawing-
master, chiefly amongst the higher classes.   He taught
the very highest, for he gave lessons to the Queen herself.   I have never had the honour of seeing any of
her Majesty's drawings, but I have had the advantage
of her criticism, and I can well believe in the reports
of the excellence of her work.*

*The story goes that one day, in the course of a
lesson, the Queen let her pencil fall to the ground.
Both master and pupil stooped to pick it up; and, to
the horror of Leitch, there was a collision—the master's
head struck that of his royal pupil! and before he
could stammer an apology, the Queen said, smiling:*

*"Well, Mr. Leitch, if we bring our heads together
in this way, I ought to improve rapidly."*

CHAPTER I.

On the 29th of August, 1817, a boy was born in London gifted with a genius which, in the short time allowed for its development, delighted and astonished the world. The child's name was Leech, and he was christened John. The Leech family was of Irish extraction. From information received, it appears that the father of Leech, also called John, was possessed of an uncle who had made a large fortune as the owner of the London Coffee-House, Ludgate Hill. With this fortune he retired, leaving his nephew to reign in his stead at the Coffee-House, not without a reasonable hope and expectation that the nephew would follow in the uncle's prosperous footsteps. But times had changed. Clubs were being formed, and the customers of the Ludgate Hill place of entertainment preferred to be enrolled as members of the novel institutions rather than subject themselves to the somewhat mixed company at the Coffee-House. Leech's establishment, however, struggled on into my early time, for I can well remember being advised, if I wished for a good and wonderfully cheap dinner, consisting—as per advertisement—of quite startling varieties of dishes, my desire might be gratified by payment of eighteen-pence to the authorities at the London Coffee-House, Ludgate Hill.

I do not know the precise time at which the doors of the Coffee-House were finally closed and the father Leech, with his large family, was thrown upon the world ; but it must have been some years after the subject of this memoir had been enrolled amongst the Charterhouse scholars, an event that took place when he was seven years old. Previous to this by about four years, some feeble buds of the genius that blossomed so abundantly afterwards are said to have shown themselves, and to have been observed by Flaxman as the child sat with pencil and paper on his mother's knee. The great sculptor is reported to have said :

" This drawing is wonderful. Do not let him be cramped by drawing-lessons ; let his genius follow its own bent. He will astonish the world."

I venture to think that for this story a grain of

salt would be by no means sufficient. No drawing done by a child of three years old, however gifted, could be "wonderful" in the estimation of Flaxman; and that such an artist as he was should have said anything so foolish as what is tantamount to advising a parent against "learning to draw" I take the liberty of disbelieving. Flaxman was a friend of the Leeches, and in after years, while John Leech was still a youth, the sculptor again examined some of his sketches, and, after looking well at them, he very likely said, as is reported:

"That boy must be an artist; he will be nothing else."

A child of seven seems almost cruelly young to be subjected to the hardships of a public school.

"I thought," wrote John's father, "that I was not wrong in sending him thus early, as Dr. Russell, the head-master, had a son of the same age in the school, and John was in the same form with him."

No doubt the elder Leech felt much the parting from his little son, but to Mrs. Leech the boy's leaving home was a severe blow; the mother's heart would no doubt realize and exaggerate the perils to mind and body arising from contact with something like six hundred fellow-pupils, scarcely

one so young, and none so loving and lovable as her
little boy. John was boarded at a house close by
the Charterhouse, and only allowed to go home
at rare intervals. The fond mother, however, could
not live without seeing him, and to enable her to
gratify her longing, a room was hired in a house
overlooking the boy's playground, from which, carefully hidden, she could see her little son as he
walked and talked with the form-fellow, "the particular friend" to whom a sympathetic nature had
attached him ; or watch him as he joined heart and
soul in some game—not too rough—for a fall from
his pony, by which his arm had been broken and was
still far from strong, made such rough sports as are
common to schoolboys too dangerous to be indulged
in.

The Charterhouse rejoiced in a drawing-master
named Burgess. Upon what principles that master
proceeded to train the youth of Charterhouse I am
unable to speak ; they were most likely those in
vogue at the time of young Leech's sojourn. If
they were of that description, it was fortunate that
Leech paid—as is said—little or no attention to
them, finding a difficulty, no doubt, in applying
them to the sketches that constantly fell from him
on to the pages of his school-books.

It may be urged that when Flaxman warned the boy's mother against teaching as being sure to cramp her son's genius, he alluded to the Burgess method. That may have been so. But a man like Flaxman, who had possessed himself by severest study as a young man of the means by which his powers were developed, would, I think, have been sure to warn Mrs. Leech of the difference between the teaching that would be mischievous, and that which is proved to be indispensable by the universal practice of the greatest painters. I am aware I shall be confronted with the case of John Leech, who was, so to speak, entirely self-taught; but Leech was not a painter, and certainly never could have become a good one without training; besides, he was altogether exceptional—unique, in fact. In my opinion, we are as likely to see another Shakespeare or Dickens as another Leech.

This is a digression, for which I apologize. I cannot find that my hero—I may call him such, for he was ever a hero to me—paid much attention to classical knowledge. Latin verses were impossible to him, but they had to be done; so, as he said, he "got somebody to do them for him." In spite of his weak arm, he fenced with Angelo, the school fencing-master; but, beyond the advantage of the exercise, the accomplishment was of no use to him.

Here I cannot resist an anecdote of which the fencing reminds me.

Some years before Leech's death the editor of a newspaper, who was remarkable for the severity of his criticisms and for his extreme personal ugliness, had made some caustic remarks on Leech's work in general, and on some special drawings in particular.

" If that chap," said Leech to me, "doesn't mind what he is about, I will *draw* and defend myself"— an idle threat, for nothing could have provoked that gentle, noble nature into personality, no trace of which is to be found in the long list of his admirable works.

Several letters, delightfully boyish, written by Leech to his father from the Charterhouse, are in my possession. Some of them, I think, may appropriately appear in this place.

" Septr 19 1826

" DEAR PAPA

" I hope you are quite well. I beg you will let me come out to see you for I am so dull here, and I am always fretting about, because I wrote to you yesterday and you would not let me come out.

I will fag hard if you will let me come out, and will you write to me, and the letter that you write put in when you are going to Esex and when you return for I want to very particularly

" How is Mamma, Brother and Sisters

" I hope Ester is quite well,

" Your affectionate

" Son

" J LEECH

" I am very sorry that I stayed away from School with —— but I promise never to do it again and I beg you will let me come out on Sunday."

"Charter House October 2 <u>1826</u>

" MY DEAR PAPA.

"You told me to write to you when the reports where made out, they are made out now, and mine is, does his Best. I hope you are quite well, and Mamma the same. I hope Tom Mary Caroline, and Ester are quite well. I have not spoken to Mr Chapman yet about the tutor, and drawing Master, because I had not an oppertunity, send me a cake as soon as it is convenient

" Your affectionate son

" J LEECH."

[*No date.*]

" My dear Papa,

"I write this note to know how poor little Polly is I hope she is better to day pray write to me before the day is over and tell me how she is. I hope you and Mamma Tom and Fanny are all well since I left you last night.

"I am happy to say I am at the very top off the Form

"Tell Mamma not to forget to come and see me on Wenesday as she said she would. I would write to Polly now only I have not time pray give Polly a 1000 kiss for me and Fanny and Tom the same. As I said before I hope poor little Polly is better.

"Your affectionate

"Son

"J Leech."

" My Dear Papa,

"My report was made out yesterday but I forgot to write to you therefore I tell you to-day, it was (generally attentive) If any afternoon or morning that you have time I should be very happy to see you. You can see me in the morning from 12 to half-past two and in the evening from 4 till 9.

" Send me another suit of clothes if you please and a cap. Mind the gloves. I hope Polly continues to get better and I hope you and Mamma Brother and sisters are quite well. Send me a penknife if you please. I remain

" Your affectionate

" Son

" J Leech."

" Dear Papa

" Will you let me come out to see you once before my sisters go to school, for I feel quite unhappy here and miserable. I am afraid I shall not be able to get promoted yet, therefore I am afraid I shant be able to come out. But you promised me that if I did not get promoted you would let me come out. I try as much as I can to get promoted. do let me come out once before my Sisters go to School.

" Your affectionate

" Son

" J Leech

" Tell Mamma to send me a cake as soon as she can

" Send me some money as soon as you can."

"September 14 1827

" My Dear Papa.

"I am happy to say that Mr Baliscombe says that for my Holiday Task I deserve promotion and says it is very well done indeed.   come and see me as soon as you can.   I think I shall get promoted when Dr Russell sees my Holiday Task—In fact Mr Baliscombe is going to ask him to put me up. I hope you and Mamma are quite well.   Springett went to the play he tells me and did not come back till the morning.   I hope dear old Camello and the dear little Baby Bunning are quite well, would you mind sending Mrs Jeffkins some partridges for I know she would like some.   Tell Mamma to write to me as soon as she possibly can.

" Your affectionate

" Son

" J Leech

" P.S.   I would not send the porter only I have got neither wafer nor seal'wax."

"Sepr 16th 1827

" My dear Papa.

"I am very happy indeed to say that I am promoted for I know it makes you happy.   let me come out next Saturday and come and see me to-morrow. I have no sealing wax or would not send the porter.

" I hope you are quite well and Mamma and Old Camello and the little Baby Bunning the same

"" Your affectionate

"" Son

"" J Leech."

"" Dear Papa

"" As I am rather short of money and want to keep my money I've got, I should be much obliged if you would give my ambassador 18 pence or so as I've promised a boy at school one of those small bladders to make balloons of, if you remember you bought me one once. I hope you are all well

"" I remain

"" Your affectionate son

"" J Leech."

"" Dear Papa

"" Will you be so kind as to send me half a crown by the porter and allowence me every week

"" I was obliged to send the porter

"" I hope you Mamma Brothers and sisters are quite well.

"" Your affectionate son

"" J Leech."

[*No date.*]

" My dear Mamma

" I understand that you came to see me yesterday, and me being in the green, you did not see me, so that made me still more unhappy, I beg you will come and see me on Saturday for I am very unhappy.

" I want to see you or Papa very much indeed.

" Your affectionate son

" J Leech."

" My dear Papa.

" You desired me to send you my report I have not had it since the last one. I went into be examined by Dr Russell yesterday but I did not get promoted but I did not lose more than one or two places. I will send you my next report. I hope you are quite well.

" Mamma and Brother and sisters the Same

" Your affectionate

" Son

" J Leech.

" I would have written to you sooner but *I had not time.*"

Leech made no way at the Charterhouse; never approaching the position held by Thackeray, who was four years his senior : indeed, I doubt that they saw, or cared to see, much of each other, little dreaming that they would ultimately become dear and fast friends till death separated them, only to meet again, as we believe, after the sad, short interval that elapsed between the deaths of each.

I cannot say I believe in inherited talent, but the fact that the elder Leech was said to be a remarkable draughtsman seems to strengthen the theory held by some people. I have never seen any specimens of the father's drawing, nor did I ever hear the son speak of it. Anyway, Leech *père* had no faith in the practice of art as a means of livelihood for his son, for he informed the youth, after a nine years' attendance at the Charterhouse, that he was destined for the medical profession. There is no record of any objection on the part of Leech to his father's decision, at which I feel surprise ; for the flame which burnt so brilliantly in after-life must have been always well alight, and very antagonistic to the kind of work required from the embryo surgeon. Leech's gentle yielding nature influenced him then as always ; and he went to St. Bartholomew's, where under Mr. Stanley, the surgeon of the hospital, he worked hard and delighted his master by his excellent anatomical drawings. From these studies may be traced, I think, much of the knowledge of the human form, and above all of *proportion*, always displayed in his work; for in those wonderful drawings, whether a figure is tall or short, fat or thin, whether he deals with a child or a giant, with a dog or a horse, no disproportion can be found.

It appears that the elder Leech's affairs were already in such an embarrassed condition, that an intention to place his son with Sir George Ballingall, an eminent Scottish doctor, was abandoned, and after a time he was placed with a Mr. Whittle, a very remarkable person, who figures under the name of Rawkins in a novel written by Albert Smith and illustrated by Leech. Smith's work, with the title of "The Adventures of Mr. Ledbury and his Friend Jack Johnson," was first published in *Bentley's Miscellany*.

"Mr. Rawkins," says Albert Smith, "was so "extraordinary a person for a medical practitioner "that, had we only read of him instead of having "known him, we should at once have put him down "as the far-fetched creation of the author's brain. "He was about eight-and-thirty years old, and of "herculean build except his legs, which were small

"in comparison with the rest of his body. But he
"thought that he was modelled after the statues of
"antiquity, and, indeed, in respect of his nose, which
"was broken, he was not far wrong in his idea—that
"feature having been damaged in some hospital
"skirmish when he was a student. His face was
"adorned with a luxuriant fringe of black whiskers,
"meeting under his chin, whilst his hair, of a similar
"hue, was cut rather short about his head, and worn
"without the least regard to any particular style or
"direction. But it was also his class of pursuits
"that made him so singular a character. Every
"available apartment in his house not actually in use
"by human beings was appropriated to the conserv-
"ing of innumerable rabbits, guinea-pigs, and ferrets.
"His areas were filled with poultry, bird-cages hung
"at every window, and the whole of his roof had
"been converted into one enormous pigeon-trap. It
"was one of his most favourite occupations to sit, on
"fine afternoons, with brandy-and-water and a pipe,
"and catch his neighbours' birds. He had very
"little private practice; the butcher, the baker, and
"the tobacconist were his chief patients, who em-
"ployed him more especially with the intention of
"working out their accounts. He derived his prin-
"cipal income from the retail of his shop, his ap-

" pointments of medical man to the police force and
" parish poor, and breeding fancy rabbits. These
" various avocations pretty well filled up his time,
" and when at home he passed his spare minutes in
" practising gymnastics—balancing himself upon one
" hand and laying hold of staples, thus keeping him-
" self at right angles to the wall, with other feats
" of strength, the acquisition of which he thought
" necessary in enabling him to support the character
" of Hercules—his favourite impersonation—with
" due effect."

It is not to be wondered at that Mr. Whittle, *alias*
Rawkins, should find that stealing his neighbours'
pigeons, together with his other unprofitable accomplishments, to say nothing of the sparseness of paying
patients, could have only one termination—bank-
ruptcy. Mr. Whittle ended his career in a public-
house, of which he became proprietor after marrying
the widow who kept it. Here he put off his coat to
his work, and in his shirt-sleeves served his customers
with beer. Leech and Albert Smith, and others of
his pupils took his beer readily, though they had
always declined to take his pills. It is said that he
was originally a Quaker, and that he died a mis-
sionary at the Antipodes.

Leech stayed but a short time with the pigeon-

fancying Whittle, whom he left to be placed under
Dr. John Cockle, afterwards Physician to the Royal
Free Hospital. Leech seems to have been a pretty
regular attendant at anatomical and other lectures,
and it goes without saying that his notes were
garnished with sketches, for which his fellow-students
sat unconsciously; and plenty of them remain to
prove the impossibility of checking an inclination so
strongly implanted in such a genuine artist as John
Leech.

CHAPTER II.

EARLY WORK.

IT was at St. Bartholomew's that Leech made
acquaintance, which soon ripened into friendship,
with Albert Smith, Percival Leigh (a future comrade
on the *Punch* Staff, and author of the " Comic
Latin Grammar," " Pips' Diary," etc.), Gilbert à
Beckett and many others, all or most of whom
served as models for that unerring pencil.

The impecunious condition of Leech senior before
John had reached his eighteenth year was such as to
make his chances of getting a living by medicine or
surgery, even if successful, so remote as to place
them beyond consideration. No doubt the elder
Leech's misfortunes were "blessings in disguise,"
for we owe to them the necessity that compelled the
younger man to devote himself to art.

The art of drawing upon wood, to which Leech in
his later years almost entirely confined himself, dates

back from very early times. Lithography, or drawing upon stone, is a comparatively modern invention,
and, until the introduction of photography, was used
for varieties of artistic reproduction. It was to that
process we owe the first published work of Leech.
The artist was eighteen years old when " Etchings
and Sketchings," by A. Pen, Esq., price 2s. plain, 3s.
coloured, was offered tremblingly to the public. The
work was in the shape of four quarto sheets, which
were covered with sketches, more or less caricatures,
of cabmen, policemen, street musicians, hackney
coachmen with their vehicles and the peculiar breed
of animal attached to them, and other varieties of
life and character common to the streets of London.
This work is now very rarely to be met with ; it con-
sisted chiefly, I believe, of characteristic heads and half-
length figures. To " Etchings and Sketchings " the
young artist added some political caricatures, also in
lithography, of considerable merit. With these, or,
rather, with the heavy stones on which they were
drawn, we may imagine the weary wanderings from
publisher to publisher ; the painful anxiety with
which the verdict, on which so much depended,
was waited for ; the hopes that brightened at a word
of commendation, only to be scattered by a few
stereotyped phrases, such as, " Ah, very clever, but

these sort of things are not in our way, you see;
there is no demand," and so on.

1836, when Leech was still a boy, saw the production of works called " The Boy's Own Series,"
" Studies from Nature," " Amateur Originals,"
" The Ups and Downs of Life ; or, The Vicissitudes
of a Swell," etc.

The delicate touch and the grasp of character
peculiar to the artist are recognised at once in many
examples.

Leech's struggle for bread for himself and others
must have been terrible at this time ; indeed, up to the
establishment of Rowland Hill's penny post, when,
by what may be called a brilliant opportunity, Leech
attracted for the first time the public attention, which
never deserted him.

The title of this book is " The Life and *Work* of
John Leech." Of the former, as I have shown, there
is little to tell ; on the latter, volumes, critical, descrip-
tive, appreciative, might be written. An artist is
destined to immortality or speedy oblivion according to his work, and it was my earnest hope, on
undertaking this memoir, that I should be able to
prove, by the finest examples of Leech's genius, that
an indisputable claim to immortality was established

for him. To a great extent I have been permitted
to do so ; but the law of copyright has debarred me
from the selection of many brilliant pictures of life
and character on which my, perhaps unreasonably
covetous, eyes had rested. The proprietors of *Punch*
and also of the copyright of most of Leech's other
works are, no doubt, properly careful of their
interests, and I can imagine their surprise at the
extent of my first demands upon their good-nature.
In my ignorance I had thought that as my object
was the honour and glory of John Leech—a feeling,
no doubt, shared by them—the treasures of *Punch*
would be spread before me, with a request that
I would help myself. I do not in the least com-
plain that I found myself mistaken. There are, no
doubt, good reasons for the limits to which I was
restricted, though I am unable to see them ; and,
granting the existence of those reasons, I should be
ungrateful if I did not express my thanks for the small
number of illustrations from *Punch* and other sources
which I am allowed to use. I confess I was delighted to find that the first few years of the existence of *Punch* were free by lapse of time from
copyright protection, and as some of Leech's best
work appears in the volumes between 1841 and
1849, I am able to show my readers further proofs

of the justice of the artist's claim to be remembered
for all time.

Leech's hatred of organ-grinding began very early
in his career.

"WANTED, BY AN AGED LADY OF VERY NERVOUS TEMPERA-
MENT, A PROFESSOR, WHO WILL UNDERTAKE TO MESMERIZE
ALL THE ORGANS IN HER STREET. SALARY, SO MUCH PER
ORGAN."

The drawing which appeared in *Punch* in 1843,
with the above title, was the first of the humorous
series that continued almost unbroken for more than
twenty years. It is pitiable to think of the long
martyrdom that Leech suffered from an abnormal
nervous organization, which ultimately made street-
noises absolute agony to him. In the illustration
the singular difference of dress in the organ-grinder
of fifty years ago and him of the present time is
noticeable, as also are the perfect expressions of
the small audience. Leech's chief contributions to
Punch at this time were the large cuts, in which
Peel, Brougham, the great Duke of Wellington, and
others, play political parts in matters that would be
of little interest to the reader of to-day, nor are the
drawings of exceptional merit.

In 1844 there appeared an irresistible little cut,

the precursor of so many admirable variations of
skating and sliding incidents.

"Now, Lobster, keep the Pot a-biling."

What could surpass the impudence of the vigorous
youngster, or the expression of the guardsman of
amused wonder as he looks down upon the audacious
imp, as Goliath might have looked upon David?

The sensation created by the first appearance of
the dwarf Tom Thumb remains vividly in my
memory. I saw him in all his impersonations; that
of Napoleon, in which he was dressed in exact
imitation of the Emperor, was very droll. The
little creature was at Waterloo, taking quantities of
snuff from his waistcoat pocket, giving his orders
for the final charge which decided his fate; and when
he saw that all was lost, his distress was terrible:
he wrung his little hands and wept copiously, amidst
the uproarious applause and laughter of the audience.
Then he was at St. Helena, and, standing on an
imaginary rock, he folded his arms, and gazed wist-
fully in the direction of his beloved France. After
a long, lingering look, he shook his little head, and
with a sigh so loud as to astonish us, he dashed the
tears from his eyes, and made his bow to the audience, some of whom affected to be shocked by the
laughter of the unthinking, and loudly expressed

their sympathy with the great man in his fall.   I
well remember the great Duke going to see the
amusing dwarf, but why Leech should have represented him in the dancing attitude, as shown in the
illustration, seems strange.   Surely a more serious
imitation of a Napoleonic attitude would have been
more telling and more comic.

The next print illustrates a paper in *Punch* called
" Physicians and General Practitioners."

" The physician almost invariably dresses in
black," says the writer, "and wears a white neck-
cloth.   He also often affects smalls and gaiters,
likewise shirt - frills " (fancy a physician in these
days thus dressed !).   He appears, no doubt very
properly, in perpetual mourning.   The general practitioner more frequently sports coloured clothes, as
drab trousers and a figured waistcoat.   With respect
to features, the Roman nose, we think, is more
characteristic of physicians ; while among general
practitioners, we should say, the more common of
the two was the snub.

The general practitioner and the physician often
meet professionally, on which occasion their interests
as well as their opinions are very apt to clash ;
whereupon an altercation ensues, which ends by the
physician telling the general practitioner that he is

an "impudent quack," and the general practitioner's
replying to the physician that he is "a contemptible
humbug."

How perfectly Leech has realized the scene for
us the drawing abundantly shows. It is, perhaps,
not too much to say that he never surpassed in

drawing, expression, and character, these two admirable figures ; full of contempt for each other, the
emotion is expressed naturally, and with due regard
to the peculiarities, widely varying, of each of the
disputants.

More years ago than I care to remember, I met
at dinner Mr. Gibson, the Newgate surgeon. At
that time an agitation was afoot respecting public
executions, the advocates maintaining that the sight
of a fellow-creature done to death acted as a deterrent on any of the sightseers who were disposed to
risk a similar fate, the objectors declaring that the
exhibition only made brutes more brutal, and was in
no way a deterrent.   As Mr. Gibson had had a long
experience of criminals and their ways, it was thought
worth while to ask his opinion of the matter in dispute.   The surgeon said that, feeling strongly on
the subject of public hanging, he had made a point
of asking persons under sentence of death if they
had ever attended executions, and he found that
over three-fourths—he told us the exact number,
but I cannot trust my memory on the point—had
witnessed the finishing of the law.   So much for the
deterrent effect.   The disgraceful scenes that took
place at the execution of the Mannings produced a
powerful letter to the press from Dickens, and an

equally powerful article in the *Daily News*, by Mr.
Parkinson. Parliament was aroused, and public
executions ceased.

The Leech drawing which follows appeared in
1845, some years before the Manning murder, and

"WHERE 'AVE WE BIN? WHY, TO SEE THE COVE 'UNG, TO BE
SURE!"

a considerable time previous to the agitation on the
subject of hanging in public. If ever a moral lesson
was inculcated by a work of art, this powerful drawing is an example. Who knows how much it may
have done towards hastening the time when those
horrible exhibitions ceased?

Is this squalid group, with debauchery and crimi-
nality in evidence in each figure, likely to be morally
impressed by the sight of a public hanging? What
are they but types of a class that always frequented
such scenes? The dreadful woman has carried her
child with her; the little creature's attenuated limbs
point to the neglect and ill-usage sure to be met
with from such parents.

To those unacquainted with the "Caudle Lectures"
by Douglas Jerrold, which appeared at this time in
Punch, I recommend the perusal of those inimitable
papers. One of their merits is their having given
occasion for an admirable drawing by Leech. Lord
Brougham was, in the eyes of *Punch* and many
others, a firebrand in the House of Lords. He was
irrepressible, contentious, and brilliant on all occa-
sions, quarrelsome in the extreme, and a thorn in
the side of whatever Government was in power
unless he was a member of it. The Woolsack, more
especially the object of his ambition, was made a
very uneasy seat to any occupant. Behold him,
then, as Mrs. Caudle — an excellent likeness —
making night hideous for the unhappy Caudle,
whose part is played by the Lord Chancellor—
Lyndhurst—while the Caudle pillow is changed into
the Woolsack.

"The Mrs. Caudle of the House of Lords."

"What do you say? *Thank heaven! you are going to enjoy the recess, and you'll be rid of me for some months?* Never mind. Depend upon it, when you come back, you shall have it again. No, I don't raise the House and set everybody by the ears; but I'm not going to give up every little privilege, though it's seldom I open my lips, goodness knows!"—"Caudle Lectures" (improved).

Whether such a scene as the following ever took place may be doubted; but that it might have

"An Eye to Business."

happened, and may happen again, there is no doubt. One meets with strange sea-side objects, and to bathe at the same time as one's tailor is within the bounds of possibility. Leech evidently thought so, hence this delightful little cut, wherein we see the creditor—evidently a tailor—improving the occasion to remind his fellow-swimmer of his little bill.   See the businesslike aspect of the one and the astonishment and alarm of the other, who in the next few vigorous strokes will place himself beyond the reach of his creditor.

Full of sympathy, as Leech was, for human suffering, and frequently as he dealt with sea-sickness, he certainly never showed the least pity for the sufferers by that miserable malady.   Its ludicrous aspect was irresistible to him, as numbers of illustrations sufficiently prove, and none more perfectly than the one introduced in this place, with the title of " Love on the Ocean," representing a couple evidently married on the morning of this tempestuous day.   " Why, oh why," I can hear the unhappy bridegroom say to himself, " did we not arrange to pass our honeymoon in some pleasant place in England, and so have avoided crossing this dreadful sea ?"   To be ill in the dear presence of—oh, horror!   And the lady is so unconscious, so serenely unconscious, of the impending catastrophe!   She enjoys the sea, and, being of a poetical turn, she thus improves the occasion :

" Oh, is there not something, dear Augustus, truly sublime in the warring of the elements ?"

Let anyone who suffers at sea fancy what it is to
be spoken to at all, when the fearful sensations, the
awful precursors of the inevitable, have full posses-

"BUT AUGUSTUS'S HEART WAS TOO FULL TO SPEAK."

sion of him, and then to suffer in the very presence
of the dear creature from whom every human weakness has been hitherto carefully hidden! The drawing is followed by a poem, in which the position of

the unhappy Augustus is described.   He could not
speak in reply to his bride's appeal ; in the words of
the poet :

> " She gazed upon the wave,
>   Sublime she declared it ;
> But no reply he gave—
>   He could not have dared it.

> " Oh, then, ' Steward !' he cried,
>   With deepest emotion ;
> Then tottered to the side,
>   And leant o'er the ocean."

Poor miserable Augustus ! his face is pale as
death, his treasured locks blown out of shape ; his
eyeglass swings in the wind ; the distant steamer is
making mad plunges into the heaving wave ; the
rain falls, and let us hope the romantic bride turns
away as her young husband "leans o'er the ocean."

Only those who have passed from the tableland of
life can recollect the passion for speculation in rail-
ways that took possession of the public in 1845 and
the two or three following years.   I myself caught
the disease, and, acting on the advice of " one who
knew," I bought a number of shares in one of the
new lines ; these were £25 shares, on which £8
each had been paid.   I was assured by my adviser
that I should receive interest at the rate of eight per
cent. till the year 1850 ; after that time the line would

pay ten. I awoke one morning to find that a panic
was in full blast, and all railway property depreciated.
My feelings may be imagined, for I certainly cannot
describe them, when I found, on reference to the
Times, that my £8 shares—£17 being still due
upon each—were quoted at half a crown apiece!
My friend had the courage of his opinions, for he
had invested the whole of his property in railway
stocks. He was completely ruined in mind and
body, and died miserably before the panic was
over.

Multiply these examples by thousands, and you
will arrive at a clear idea of the nature of a panic,
which seems to mystify the young gentleman
immortalized by Leech in the drawing illustrating
the following dialogue :

" I SAY, JIM, WHAT'S A PANIC ?"

" BLOWED IF I KNOW ; BUT THERE IS VON TO BE SEEN IN THE
CITY."

It has been my fate in the course of a long life to
attend several fancy-dress balls, but I can scarcely
call to mind a single example of the successful
assumption of an historical character, or, indeed, of
any character that could disguise the very modern
young lady or gentleman who was masquerading in
it. My first acquaintance with Mark Lemon, so

long the esteemed editor of *Punch*, began in the
Hanover Square Rooms, at a fancy-dress ball given
by a society—chiefly, I think, composed of the better
class of tradespeople—called the Gothics.   On that
occasion might have been seen a young gentleman
in the dress of one of Charles II.'s courtiers, and
looking about as unlike his prototype as possible—in
earnest conversation with another courtier, of the
time of George II.   I was of the Charles' period,
Lemon of that of the Georges.   Those who remember Lemon's figure later in life would have been
surprised by the change that time had made in it,
if they could have witnessed the interview between
the two young men, one scarcely stouter than the
other.   In proof of my idea that the greater number
of guests were in trade, I might give scraps of conversation between Mary Queen of Scots and Guy
Fawkes, or between Henry VIII. and Edward the
Black Prince, that would leave no doubt on the
subject ; nay, later in the evening I had convincing
proof of the correctness of my surmise, as you shall
hear.   I danced with a Marie Antoinette of surpass-
ing beauty, with whom I fell incontinently in love.
More than once I danced with her, and when
supper was announced, my earnest appeal to be
allowed to conduct her to the banquet was suc-

cessful. My lovely friend was full of the curiosity peculiar to her sex, which showed itself in her anxiety to know who and what I was. To tell the truth, I was equally curious to know who she was, and what her friends were.

" Well," said I, " if you will tell me who you are, I will tell you who I am and what I am."

" Oh," was the reply, " I think I know what you are ; but what's your name ?"

" You know what I am ?" said I, surprised; "what am I ?"

" Well, you are in the same line that we are, I fancy."

" And what line is that ?"

" The army tailoring. Am I right ?"

In the illustration that accompanies these remarks Leech has succeeded in presenting to us a Norman knight completely characteristic, a Crusader more real, I think, than any modern could have rendered him. The lady he escorts, in a dress a few hundred years after Crusading times, is very lovely. The capital little Marchioness, with the big door-key, the four-wheeler, and the laughing crowd, make up a scene of inimitable humour.

We now come to the first of those precocious

youths in whose mannish ways, whose delightful
impertinence to their elders, whose early susceptibility to the passion of love for ladies three times
older than themselves, are shown by Leech in
many a scene I should have given to my readers,

"Sir! Please, Mr.! Sir! you've forgot the Door-key!"

but over them the Copyright Act stands guard.
"'Tis true, 'tis pity, pity 'tis, 'tis true," that in a
book intended solely to do honour to Leech's
genius, so many of the most perfect examples
of it are denied to us.

Well may the governor stare with open-mouthed

astonishment at such a proposal from such a creature !
Look at him as he throws his little arm over his
chair in the swaggering attitude he has so often
observed in his elders, and raises a full glass of
claret !　"Just as the twig is bent the tree's inclined ;" but that we know that in this instance the

"ETON BOY (*loq.*) : "Come, governor ! just one toast—'The
Ladies'!"

twig is indulging in a harmless freak, one might be
inclined to dread the tree's inclining.

The political opinions of the writer of this book
are of no consequence to himself or anybody else.
It would perhaps be pretty near the truth if he were
to admit that he had no political opinions worth
speaking of.　To those, however, who were in-
terested in the struggle for Free Trade, which in the

year 1846 raged with great fury, the question was,
and still is, one of vital interest. The landed interest,
headed by most of the aristocracy on the one side,
and the manufacturing interest, championed by
Cobden and Bright, on the other, raised a storm in
which language the reverse of parliamentary was
tossed from side to side. Peel was Prime Minister,
and his ultimate conversion to the principles of Free
Trade, and consequent advocacy of the repeal of
the Corn Laws, horrified his supporters—by whom,
notably by Disraeli, he became the object of en-
venomed attack—but led to a settlement of the
question, and gave Leech an opportunity for the
production of drawings of the victor and the van-
quished, entitled, Cobden's "Bee's Wing" and Richmond's "Black Draught," two of the most successful
of the political cartoons.

"The Brook Green Volunteer" gave Leech the
opportunity for many illustrations which, to my
mind, are nearer approaching caricature than most
of his work; nor have they, as a rule, the beauty or
human interest that so many of his drawings show.
I fear I must charge the volunteer himself with
being in possession of an impossible face and a no
less impossible figure; his action also is exaggerated.
In compensation we have a delightful family group.

The mother with that naked baby perambulating her person is beyond all praise. Women do strange things, but I deny the possibility of such a woman as Leech has drawn ever finding it in her heart to marry that volunteer. The little thing standing on tip-toe to dabble in baby's basin for the benefit of her doll, the delighted lookers-on, not forgetting the warrior riding his umbrella into action, are invested with the charm that Leech, and Leech only, could give them.

The year 1846 gave birth to the first fruit from a field in which Leech found such a bountiful harvest. The racecourse gave opportunities for the exhibition of life and character of which the great artist took advantage in numberless delightful examples. Pen and pencil record adventures by road and rail. Whether the excursionist is going to the Derby or returning from it, whether he is high or low, a Duke or a costermonger, that unerring hand is ready to note his follies or his excesses, always with a kindly touch, or to point a moral if a graver opportunity presents itself.

A madman, they say, thinks all the world mad but himself; and it is not uncommon for a drunken man to imagine himself to be the only sober person in the company. That some feeling of this kind possesses

the rider in the drawing opposite, as he addresses
the stolid postboy, is evident enough ; his drunken
smile, his battered hat, and his dishevelled dress, are
eloquent of his proceedings on the course ; and if his
return from the Derby is not signalized by a fall
from his horse, he will be more fortunate than he
deserves to be.   In works of art the value of contrast is well known, and a better example than the
face of the postboy offers to that of his questioner
could not be imagined.   He drunk, indeed ! not a
bit of it.

A pretty creature in the background must not be
overlooked.   She is a perfect specimen of Leech's
power of creating beauty by a few pencil-marks.
Her beauty has evidently attracted notice, and
caused complimentary remarks from · passers-by,
which are resented by the old lady in charge,
who tells the speaker to "*go on with his imper-
dence !*"

I cannot resist presenting my readers with another
Derby sketch.   It is more than probable that if
either of these young gentlemen had asked for leave
of absence from his official duties for the purpose
of going to the Derby, he would have met with
stern denial.   The attraction, however, is irresistible,
and though the subterfuge by which it is achieved is

"THE RETURN FROM THE DERBY."

SMITH : " Hollo ! Poster, ain't you precious drunk, rather ?"   POSTBOY : " Drunk ! not a bit of it !"

not to be defended, who is there that is not glad that
the wicked boy is penning that audacious letter, as it
is the cause of our having a picture that is a joy
for ever?   As a work of art, whether as a composi-

"THE DERBY EPIDEMIC."

tion of lines and light and shadow, in addition to
perfect character and expression, this drawing takes
rank amongst the best of Leech's works.   Note the
admirable action of the youth who is putting on his

coat—a momentary movement caught with consummate skill.

"GENTLEMEN,

"Owing to sudden and very severe indisposition, I regret to say that I shall not be able to attend the office to-day. I hope, however, to be able to resume my duties to-morrow.

"I am, gentlemen,

"Yours very obediently,

"PHILLIP COX."

Doctors differ, as everybody knows; and in no opinion do they differ more than in the way children should be treated. One of the faculty will tell you that a healthy child should be allowed to eat as much as he or she likes; another advises that as grown-up people are disposed to eat a great deal more than is good for them, a boy is pretty sure to do the same unless a wholesome check is imposed upon his unruly appetite. A great authority is reported to have said that as many people are killed by over-eating as by over-drinking; "in fact," said he, "they dig their graves with their teeth." If that be so, the young gentleman in "Something like a Holiday" is destined for an early tomb.

Comment on this wonderful youth is needless.

We can only share the alarm and astonishment so admirably expressed in the pastrycook's face. That this awful juvenile's memory should serve him so

PASTRYCOOK : "What have you had, sir ?"
BOY : "I've had two jellies ; seven of those, and eleven of these ; and six of those, and four bath-buns ; a sausage-roll, ten almond-cakes, and a bottle of ginger-beer."

perfectly when he has taken such pains to cloud it, as well as every other faculty, is also surprising.

If "a fellow-feeling makes us wondrous kind," the
boy in the following drawing would have delighted
in the society of the *gourmet* at the pastrycook's.
Boiled beef and gooseberry-pie are good things

"ALARMING SYMPTOMS ON EATING BOILED BEEF AND
GOOSEBERRY-PIE."

LITTLE BOY: "Oh lor, ma! I feel just exactly as if my jacket
was buttoned."

enough in their way, but one may have too much
of a good thing, with the inevitable result of the
tightening of the jacket. This greedy-boy drawing

appeared in 1846, and created a great sensation in
the youth of that day, and many days since.   Careful parents have been known to use this terrible
example of over-eating as a warning to their offspring that a fit of apoplexy frequently followed the
tightening of the jacket.

I think my married reader of the rougher sex
will agree with me when I say that there are few
more uncomfortable, not to say alarming, moments
than those spent in the awful interview with the
parents of his beloved, during which he has to
prove beyond all doubt that he is in every respect
an individual to whom the happiness of a "dear
child" can be safely entrusted.   What a bad quarter
of an hour that is before the meeting, when he has
grave doubts as to the sufficiency of his income!
Will it, with other future possibilities, be considered
sufficient to assure to "my daughter, sir, the com-
forts to which she has been accustomed"?   This he
will have to answer satisfactorily, together with a
few score more questions more or less agonizing.
Leech drew a scene of common application when
he produced the picture that follows, which he calls
"Rather Alarming"—"On Horror's Head, Horrors
accumulate."   Look at that terrible female and pros-
pective mother-in-law!—think of satisfying such a

woman that you are worthy of admission into her
family! How sincerely one pities that poor little
Corydon, and how heartily one wishes him success!

"Rather Alarming."

LADY: "You wished, sir, I believe, to see me respecting the
state of my daughter's affections with a view to a matrimonial
alliance with that young lady. If you will walk into the library,
my husband and I will discuss the matter with you."

YOUNG CORYDON: "Oh, gracious!"

Leech treats—how admirably!—another greedy
boy, or, rather, two greedy boys.

JACKY: "Hallo, Tommy! what 'ave you got there?"
TOMMY: "Hoyster!"
JACKY: "Oh, give us a bit!"

A Calais oyster, no doubt—large enough for
both; but Tommy will not share his happiness.
Intensity of expression pervades him from his open
mouth to his fingers' ends. Jacky's face and figure
are no less expressive of eagerness to join in the
banquet.

If ever man suffered from *embarras de richesse*, I
am that individual in making a selection from the
early drawings of Leech; where all, or nearly all,
are so perfect, choice becomes difficult indeed. I
cannot resist, however, the one that follows this
remark. For perfection of character and richness
of humour, it seems to me unsurpassable. The

doctor's attitude as he contemplates his victim—who
seems to have brought with her the huge empty
physic-bottles to prove that she has taken all her

"So you have taken all your Stuff, and don't feel any
better, eh? Well, then, we must alter the Treat-
ment. You must get your Head shaved; and if you
will call here to-morrow Morning about eleven, my
Pupil will put a Seton in the back of your Neck."

"stuff"—to say nothing of his startling individuality,
is Nature itself; and that immortal pupil with the
big knife, smiling in anticipation of the operation

"to-morrow about eleven"! One can read on the
face of the patient a dull realization of the doctor's
announcement that only a seton in the back of her
neck—whatever that may mean to her—will be of

"Awful Apparition to a Gentleman whilst Shaving in
the Edgware Road, September 29, 1846."

any service now ; and to render the operation
successful, she must have her head shaved.

The statue of the Duke of Wellington, which so
long disgraced Hyde Park Corner, has disappeared,

to the satisfaction of the world in general, though
there were, I believe, a few dissentients who saw,
or said they saw, beauty in one of the most hideous
objects ever perpetrated by the hand of man ; yet
the "ayes had it," and the monster has departed.

The effigy was manufactured in a studio near
Paddington Green, and it was on its journey
through the Edgware Road to the arch now on
Constitution Hill that the gentleman in Leech's
cartoon was startled by a very remarkable object, to
say the least of it.

Speaking from my own experience, I have always
found a difficulty in giving the effect of wind in a
picture ; the action of it on drapery, trees, skies,
etc., is—from the almost momentary nature of the
gusts—far from an easy task. No one who ever
handled a brush or a pencil has been so successful
as Leech in conveying the action of wind on every
object, and never did he succeed more completely
than in an " Awful Scene on the Chain Pier at
Brighton," which is, no doubt, somewhat farcical ;
but how intensely funny ! Master Charley has
gone, and his ma's parasol has accompanied him.
The horror-struck nursemaid is almost blown off her
feet ; and Charley's brother, also terror-stricken, will
be down on his back in a moment ; whilst his little

sister maintains her equilibrium with great difficulty. The flying hat, and the couple staggering against the blast in the distance, all help to realize for us the exact effect of a wind-storm.

NURSEMAID : "Lawk ! there goes Charley, and he's took his ma's parasol ! What *will* missus say ?"

As there is no condition in life that has not proved food for Leech's pencil, that of the waiter

WAITER : "Gent in No. 4 likes a holder and a thinner wine, does he ? I wonder how he'll like this bin !"

was fruitful in many never-to-be-forgotten scenes. I introduce one which is very humorous, and scarcely an exaggeration. It is called " How to Suit the

Taste." A guest seems to have found his port too new and strong.

One of the peculiarities of Leech's art is that " time cannot wither it, nor custom stale its infinite variety." I defy the most serious Scotchman to look at the sketch below without laughing at it. As the gentleman who is on the highroad to being

"HOLLO! HI! HERE, SOMEBODY! I'VE TURNED ON THE HOT WATER, AND I CAN'T TURN IT OFF AGAIN!"

parboiled is in one of the sketches of 1846, many of my readers may see him for the first time. I envy that man; but though I am very familiar with the wonderful little drawing, a renewed acquaintance is always a delight to me. We know the bather can jump out of the scalding water when he likes, but there he is, with clouds of steam rising about

him, screaming in deadly terror for "somebody" to
come to his rescue.

Here follows a drawing of a different character,

"SYMPTOMS OF A MASQUERADE."

BETTER-HALF (*loq.*) : "Is this what you call sitting up with a
sick friend, Mr. Wilkins?"

opening up very appreciable possibilities, and not
very pleasant consequences for the hero of the
piece. Mr. Wilkins left the domestic hearth to sit
up with a sick friend. "Yes, my dear," I can hear

him say to his spouse, " I may be late ; for if I find
I can comfort the poor fellow by my conversation, I
cannot find it in my heart to hurry away from him."
Wicked Mr. Wilkins! What was there wrong in
going to a masquerade? and if it was criminal to
do so, why leave the evidence of your guilt where
Mrs. W. could find it? Was that a *lady's* mask?
In the eyes of the outraged wife I dare say it was,
though it may only have been used to cover the
homely features of the deceiver, whose pale face
and empty soda-water bottle plainly prove that the
evening's entertainment will not bear the morning's
reflections.

The first drawings of " The Rising Generation,"
in which are portrayed the premature affections and
the amusing affectations of the manners and sayings
of their elders that, according to Leech, distinguished
the *jeunesse doré* of England, appeared in 1846, and
have been so admirably described by Dickens elsewhere as to leave me only the task of placing some
of the drawings before the reader, carefully avoiding
those the great writer has noticed so felicitously.
The young gentleman in the drawing introduced
here would like to catch the pretty creature talking
to the fascinating young man under the mistletoe, no
doubt! We know his wicked intentions; but how

would he carry them out? He is not tall enough
to reach the lady's elbow ; but love in such passionate natures laughs at difficulties, and he will find a

JUVENILE : "I say, Charley, that's a jeuced fine gurl talking to
young Fipps! I should like to catch her under the mistletoe."

way ; and he calls a man old enough to be his father
young Fipps! Delightful little dog! and no less
delightful is his friend Charley, who smiles encouragement, and would do likewise. These works

of Leech possess what it is not too much to call an
historical interest, as they chronicle truly the dresses
of the time. In the object of our young friend's

JUVENILE : " Uncle !"

UNCLE : " Now, then, what is it ? This is the fourth time
you've woke me up, sir."

JUVENILE : " Oh ! just put a few coals on the fire and pass the
wine, that's a good old chap !"

admiration, I fancy I see the approach of crinoline,
while her ringlets afford a striking contrast to the
fringes of the present day. An old lady would now

create a sensation indeed if she appeared in a turban
like that which bedecks the sitting figure.

Again the irrepressible juvenile, under different
conditions. Behold him practising upon a very
testy old gentleman, who has been so rude, in the
estimation of his young nephew, as to go to sleep
after dinner.

"THE RISING GENERATION."

JUVENILE: "Ah, it's all very well! Love may do for boys and
gals; but we, as men of the world, know 'ow 'ollow it is."

In his notices of the freaks of the rising generation Leech did not confine himself to juveniles of
the higher and middle ranks, but occasionally he
shows us the young snob, of whom he makes—with

modifications—the same mannish and amusingly vain
creature as his confrères, the little swells. As an
illustration, I present my reader with a scene in a
coffee-house, in which two friends are refreshing
themselves, and exchanging philosophical reflections
on the vanities of human life. These lads look like
shop-boys, but—in their own estimation—with souls
far above their positions in life. The spokesman
has found the truth of the poet's description of the
course of true love in the conduct of some barmaid
who has jilted him, hence his bitterness.

In the year 1847 Leech produced much of his
best work, and in justification of this dictum I advise
the study of a drawing full of character, humour, and
beauty. Thousands of heads of households could
vouch for the truth of the situation depicted there,
and where is the mistress whose mind has not mis-
given her when a request from her pretty servant
has been urged that she might "go to chapel this
evening"? "Chapel, indeed!" one can hear her
mutter to herself; "I've not the least doubt the
baker's man is waiting for her round the corner!"
I am loath to find fault with such a work as this,
but I *do* think that perfect maid deserved a more
presentable lover than the pudding-faced, knock-
kneed soldier who is personating the "bit of ribbin."

The artist appears to me to charge his story-telling maid with very bad taste indeed. Would the drawing have lost, or gained, if Leech had given us a handsome young guardsman instead of this ugly fellow? He would, at any rate, have made the little fib a little more pardonable. The other figures deserve careful attention—notably, the youth absorbed in the study of natural history.

SERVANT-MAID: "If you please, mem, could I go out for half an hour to buy a bit of ribbin, mem?"

If there be amongst my readers any who are unfamiliar with Cruikshank's illustrations of "Oliver Twist," I advise them to turn to them, where they will find a drawing of Fagin in the condemned cell at Newgate, one of the most awful renderings of agonized despair ever depicted by the hand of an artist. This great work is travestied by Leech in a manner so admirable as to make the travesty take rank with the original. Instead of Fagin, see King Louis Philippe smarting under the failure of his schemes and the impending fall of his dynasty. By the Spanish marriages the veteran trickster destroyed the power which he sought to consolidate.

Domestic troubles and misadventures were represented by Leech in many examples, with a sympathetic humour that never wearies. A party may

be assembled for a dinner which is strangely delayed ;
conversation flags into silence. The host and
hostess become uneasy, when a button-boy appears
with the ominous "Oh, if you please, 'm, cook's very
sorry, 'm, could she speak to you for a moment?"
Something has happened ; but we are left in un-
certainty as to what it was.

Or the dinner is served, when an alarming announcement is made :

SERVANT (*rushing in*): "Oh, goodness gracious, master!
There's the kitchen chimley afire, and two parish ingins a-knock-
ing at the street door."

One of the happiest of the servant-gal-isms appears
this year—the precursor of many excellent tunes on
the same string—delightfully illustrative of the
vanity which we all share, more or less, with our
maids. In the picture that follows, the sight of the
old lady's new bonnet and a convenient looking-
glass have provided an opportunity that the pretty
servant could not resist. She must see how she
looks in it—and behold the result!

I must refer my readers to *Punch's* almanac for
1848, copiously illustrated by Leech, for many
admirable examples of his many-sided powers.
Alas! my space forbids the reproduction of any of
them. Amongst the rest there is one of a gentle-

man suffering from influenza, which, by the way, seems to have been as prevalent in 1848 as it has been recently, though not so fatal in its effects.

DOMESTIC (*soliloquizing*) : " Well, I'm sure, missis had better give this new bonnet to me, instead of sticking such a young-looking thing upon her old shoulders." (The impudent minx has immediate warning.)

Our sufferer is visited by a condoling friend : he sits with his feet in hot water, and, with his hand on the bell-pull, he says, " This is really very kind of

you to call.   Can I offer you anything ?   A basin
of gruel, or a glass of cough mixture ?   Don't say
no !"

Another of a rich old lady, who stands before a
pyramid of oyster-barrels, all sent to her at Christmas by her poor relations.   Another—but I must
pause, and again refer my reader to the almanac.

I find yet one more of the " Rising Generation "
series quite irresistible.   The two little bucks are
perfect, and the idea of such a report as that one of
them was engaged to the magnificent woman—whose
face we long to see—is so ludicrous as almost to reach
the sublime of absurdity.   Look at the eagerness
with which the precocious youth impresses upon his
friend the necessity of contradicting the rumour,
and the well-bred and considerate way in which the
friend receives a communication which does not
surprise him.   He does not smile at it.   There is
nothing astonishing in a man's being in love with
such a fine woman, and he will certainly contradict
anyone who repeats the report, as his friend desires.
If the creatures had been six feet high instead of
not so many more inches, they could not have
conducted themselves more naturally.

1848 witnessed the fall of the French throne and
the tottering of others in Europe.   It was a terrible

time, and though the English throne was safe enough, a great deal of vague alarm existed in this country. The Chartists met in their thousands, and

JUVENILE: "Oh, Charley, if you hear a report that I am going to be married to that girl in black, you can contradict it. There's nothing in it."

prepared a bill of grievances with signatures, making a document, it was said, some miles long. This petition they announced their intention of presenting to Parliament, accompanied by a procession, which

was really to be some miles long ; but they reckoned
without their host—of opponents. Special constables
were enrolled (amongst whom was Louis Napoleon),
soldiers were at hand, skilfully hidden by the great
Duke, and the Chartist procession was peacefully
stopped long before it got to Westminster.

There were firebrands then as now, and a meeting
was called by one of them to be held in Trafalgar
Square—see how history repeats itself!—where a
ragamuffin assembly appeared ; so did the police,
and nothing came of it except a few broken heads
and the inimitable drawings by Leech. How admirable they are !

The person who wanted more liberty, equality,
and fraternity than was good for him or anybody
else, was a Mr. Cochran, and his adherents were
called Cochranites.

COCHRANITE : " Hooray ! Veeve ler liberty !! Harm your-
selves !! To the palis !! Down with heverythink !!!!"

In the second picture the Cochranite has col-
lapsed. A stalwart policeman has taken him in
hand, and he cries, "Oh, sir—please, sir—it ain't
me, sir. I'm for God save the Queen and Rule
Britannier. Boo-hoo!—oh dear ! oh dear !" (bursts
into tears).

Below we have another result of the agitation, touched in Leech's happiest manner. A special constable endeavours to arrest an agitator, who evidently objects, and prepares for resistance.

SPECIAL CONSTABLE: "Now mind, you know—if I kill you, it's nothing; but if you kill me, by Jove! it's murder!"

A certain Master Jackey was a great favourite of Leech's. In an elaborate work this youth's pranks are chronicled under the heading of " Home for the Holidays." Whether the hero of those adventures

is the same as he who is pictured in the work I
present to my readers I know not.   In all probability the taste for practical joking which flourished
so vigorously in the holiday scenes began, as we
see, in the nursery.   Master Jackey has been to the
play, where he has witnessed the performances of a
contortionist, and, emulous of rivalling the professor,
he perils the limbs and lives of his brothers and
sisters in his operations.   We know of the tendency
to imitate in all children, but when the propensity
shows itself in the imitation of tricks that require
long practice before they can be performed with
safety, the game, though amusing to the players,
may be very dangerous to the played upon.   It is to
be hoped that the rush of the terrified mother in
this capital scene may be in time to save the baby
from a perilous fall.   The little brothers have already
tasted the consequence of Master Jackey's imitation.

The accompanying drawing was suggested by myself during an after-dinner conversation at a friend's
house.   The talk had turned on the difficulty that the
pronunciation of certain words would prove to one
who had dined not wisely but too well, when it occurred
to me that "Plesiosaurus" or "Ichthyosaurus" would
be troublesome, and I said so.   Leech smiled, and

said nothing, but in *Punch* of the week following his idea of the difficulty appeared.

" Recreations in Natural History."

First Naturalist : " What, the s-s-she-sherpent a-an (hic !) Ich-(hic :)-thyosaurus ! Nonshence !"

Second Naturalist : " Who said Ich-(hic !)-Ichthy-o-saurus ? I said Plesi-o-(hic !)-saurus plainenuff."

The cabman who doesn't know his way about London is exceptional, but he is met with occasion-

ally, and very provoking he is ; but to have his little
trap-door knocked off its hinges because he takes a
wrong turning is a punishment in excess of his fault.
The young gentleman passenger is of an impatient
turn, and he will find that his impatience will have

"CABMAN IS SUPPOSED TO HAVE TAKEN A WRONG TURNING,
THAT'S ALL."

to be paid for unless the cabman is more good-
natured than he looks.

Flunkeiana cannot be omitted in this short
summary of Leech's work, more especially as the
first of a long series is one of the best. Nothing
can be conceived more perfect than the man and the

maid at the seaside—the girl, French from top
to toe ; the flunkey, a most perfect type of the
class.

FRENCH MAID : "You like—a—ze—seaside—M'sieu Jean
Thomas ?"

JOHN THOMAS : "Par bokhoo, mamzelle—par bokhoo. I've—
aw—been so accustomed to—aw—gaiety in town, that I'm—aw
—a'most killed with arnwee down here."

The immortal Briggs made his first appearance in
Punch in the year 1849, and with one or two records
of his career I regret to say I must close my selected
list of Leech's early works. To say I regret this is
to say little, for I am obliged to forego numberless
delightful works, many as good as, and some perhaps
better than, those I have presented to my readers.
Mr. Briggs first appears with newspaper in hand in
his snug breakfast-room, listening to a complaint
from the housemaid that a slate is off the roof, and
the servant's bedroom in danger of being flooded.
Mr. Briggs replies that the sooner it is put to rights
the better, before it goes any further—and he will see
about it. Mr. Briggs does see about it ; he sees the
builder, who tells him that "a little compo" is all
that is wanted. The drawings show that eight or
ten men are required to manage the little compo,
much to Mr. Briggs' astonishment.

In the next scene a huge scaffolding is raised, and
a small army of labourers are at work on Mr. Briggs's
roof. A noise enough to wake the dead has awoke
Mr. Briggs at the unpleasant hour of five in the
morning. Flower-pots and bricks fall past his
dressing-room window. He finds "no time has
been lost, and that the workpeople have already
commenced putting the roof to rights." The builder
would not be true to his craft if he did not improve
the occasion and show his employer how easy, now
that the workpeople were about, it would be to make
certain additions in the shape of a conservatory, etc.,
to the house. Briggs weakly listens to the voice of
the charmer ; walls are battered down to enlarge the
dining-room, and the entrance-hall is enlarged. Mr.
Briggs's health gives way, and he calls in the doctor,
who prescribes horse exercise.

I think it was at one of those never-to-be-forgotten dinners at Egg's that, the talk having turned
upon shooting experiences, Dickens said that the
sudden rising of a cock-pheasant under one's nose
was like a firework let off in that uncongenial
locality. The following week Leech subjected
Mr. Briggs to the startling experience so admirably
recorded in the drawing which faces this page.

For a further acquaintance with Mr. Briggs's per-

formances on horseback, as well as his escapades with gun and fishing-rod, I must content myself with referring those curious on the matters to the pages of *Punch*, where they will find entertainment that is inexhaustible.

CHAPTER III.

MR. PERCIVAL LEIGH AND LEECH.

IN the death of Mr. Percival Leigh, which took place a short time ago, the last member of the original staff of *Punch* passed away. Mr. Leigh never married, and died at a very advanced age. I frequently met him in society, where his refined and gentle manners, and his quaintly humorous conversation, were what might have been anticipated from the author of " Pips his Diary," the " Comic Grammars," and other contributions to the paper to which he was so long and so faithfully attached. From the days of their fellow - studentship at St. Bartholomew's (with a short interval), to the time of Leech's death, a firm friendship existed between these two distinguished men.

Much alike in their sense of humour, they also resembled each other in numberless amiable qualities of heart and mind. Leigh's pen was as free from

personality, and as conspicuous for the gentleness
with which it dealt with folly, as Leech's pencil.   In
early and late days, when Leech was in trouble,
Leigh's was the hand—amongst others—ever ready
to help ; and to those who can read between the lines
in the paper which Mr. Leigh has contributed to
this book, there will be little difficulty in discovering
the " friend " who found purchasers for work that
the producer was barred (in a double sense) from
selling for himself.

I see little or no reason for weakening my asser-
tion that Leech arrived at his supreme eminence
without any art education ; for the slight mechanical
knowledge of the art of drawing upon wood which
he acquired from Mr. Orrin Smith, a wood-engraver,
is no more worthy the name of art-teaching, than the
few lessons in etching given to Leech by George
Cruikshank can be called art-education.   Following
the example of Sir John Millais, Mr. Percival Leigh
(to whom, it will be remembered, Millais recom-
mended my predecessor, Mr. Evans, to apply) furnished the following remarks for this memoir.

Said Mr. Leigh : " Orrin Smith has been dead
many years.   How long Leech was with him I
cannot say precisely.   Perhaps a twelvemonth or
thereabouts.   Smith was a sociable and rather a

clever man, but according to Leech, occasionally so economical that he would now and then try to get a little gratuitous work out of him. On one occasion Smith asked him to introduce a few figures, so as to put a touch of action into a drawing on wood, meant to illustrate a serious little book, the work of a clergyman. The scene represented was a quiet churchyard. Leech improved it with a group of little boys larking and boxing.

"Of course these embellishments, on discovery, were objected to as painfully incongruous, and had to be cancelled. I forget whether or no they had been actually engraven before they were taken out."

Thus far Mr. Leigh. I think I can interpret the incongruity. I fancy I can hear Leech say, after previous unrequited sketches, "Oh, hang it! this is too bad. Well, here goes; he shall have a few figures, and I hope he'll like 'em."

Mr. Leigh continues: "The post-office envelope was one of Leech's successes; so were the 'Comic Histories' of England and Rome, and the 'Comic Blackstone'; but his growth in popularity was gradual. He had previously illustrated 'Jack Brag' for Bentley, and subsequently various articles for *Bentley's Miscellany*, particularly the 'Ingoldsby

Legends,' as well as other ephemeral works of the
same publisher; amongst them the 'Comic Latin'
and 'English' Grammars, and the 'Children of the
Mobility,' a travesty of the 'Children of the Nobility,'
long since out of print.   He also furnished coloured
illustrations to the 'Fiddle-Faddle Fashion-book,' a
whimsical satire on the fopperies and literary
absurdities of the period, also out of print."

I venture again to interrupt the current of
Mr. Leigh's narrative with a word or two on the
" Fiddle-Faddle " book.   A copy of it, date 1840,
has been lent to me.   The literary portion, consisting mainly of a thrilling story of brigand life, the
blood-curdling tenor of which may be imagined from
the title, "Grabalotti the Bandit; or, The Emerald
Monster of the Deep Dell," is the work of Mr.
Leigh.   The story opens thus :

" Italia! oh, Italia! blooming birthplace of
beauty! land of lazzaroni and loveliness! clime
of complines and cruelty, of susceptibility and sacrilege, of roses and revenge! thy bright, blue,
boundless skies serene I love; thy verdant vales,
volcanoes, vines, and virgins!   Thy virgins? ay,
thy bright-eyed, dark-haired virgins.   I love them—
how I love them, though mine, alas! they ne'er
can be!   And there was one who, in earlier, happier

hours, before these locks were—no matter. Let
me proceed with the calmness becoming a narrator
with my tale."

And he proceeds "with a vengeance" to let us
know that the spokesman of the above is an artist
who had "halted in a deep ravine in the Abruzzi
(where, on each side, the cliffs frowned like fiends
upon the quailing traveller) to transfer to my port-
able sketch-book a slight souvenir of the celestial
scene. Absorbed in my enthralling occupation, I
heeded not the approach of a visitant; it was therefore with surprise, not unmingled with alarm, that I
was aroused by a tap upon the shoulders, accompanied by the following sarcastic greeting :

"'Is thy maternal parent, young man, aware of
thine absence from home?'

"'Quite so,' I replied, in a tremulous tone,
anxiously glancing round to behold the speaker.

"My acquaintance with literature—to say nothing
of my constant attendance at the opera—at once convinced me that I was in the hands of a brigand."

Had there been "any possible doubt whatever,"
it would have been instantly dispelled ; for after
"smiling in demoniacal derision," the disturber of
the sketcher said, "deliberately and tranquilly, as
he levelled a pistol at my head :

" ' Thy wealth or thy existence !'

" My sole remaining ducat was offered in vain. At the shrill sound of his whistle the crags bristled with bandits, and fifty carbines were pointed at my person. Blue with boiling agony, I made as a last resource the Masonic sign. It succeeded. At another signal every carbine was lowered, and breathless expectation brooded over the heart of its bearer."

The bandits, however, were not so easily satisfied ; for " a murmur of impatience, mingled with discontent, arose, like the billows of emotion, amongst the troop, and some twenty weapons again kissed with their stocks as many manly shoulders.

" ' Back, slaves, for your lives !' shouted the infuriated Grabalotti, throwing himself in front of me. ' One moment more, and, by the blood-stained power of the thundering Avalanche, the foremost of you dies !'

" Cowering in cream-like humility, each individual reversed his implement of death—all but one. A ball from the pistol of Grabalotti instantly crashed through his brain. For a moment he writhed in sable pangs ; then all was over, and darkness mantled over his impetuosity for ever. Then, turning towards me, the brigand chief gave me a civil invitation to spend the day with him, which, under existing circumstances, I thought it best to accept. On our way I took the opportunity thus furnished me to survey my lawless companion. He was at least six feet and a half, independent of the coverings of his feet, in height ; his air was stern and commanding ; raven ringlets clustered down to his shoulders. Premature intensity glowed in his volcanic eyes ; his nose was Roman, and he wore mustachios. The lines in the lower part of his face were indicative of death - fraught concentration ; and the teeth, frequently disclosed by his smile of pervading bitterness, were remarkably white. The gloom of his conical hat was mocked by gay ribands. He wore a jacket of green velvet (an expensive article), lustrously gemmed with gold buttons ; and those portions of his dress for which our language has no proper appellation were richly meandered with superior lace. His legs were variously swathed in the manner so characteristic of his profession. The carbine that slept in a snowy belt at his back ; the pistols bickering in his girdle ; and the stiletto reposing, like candid innocence, in its silver sheath, with its ivory handle protruding from his sash, were all of the most ornamental and valuable description."

This extraordinary robber and the artist arrive at

"the dwelling of the bandit, which was eligibly situate among the most romantic scenery."

Signor Grabalotti conducted his visitor to a "table groaning with fruit, and supporting six sacramental chalices filled with the richest wine."

The brigand has made a great haul of prisoners, whose friends have not shown the alacrity in rescuing them required by their captor, who, by way of entertaining his guest, orders them all, to the amount of a dozen, into his presence, and, arranging them in a row "along a trench in the background," with the assistance of twelve of his men, has them all shot.

"Almost ere the smoke had cleared away, the earth was shovelled over the bodies.

"'And now,' said the chief, 'for a dance in honour of our guest.'

"Four-and-twenty brisk young bandits, clad in jackets, green array, were instantly joined by as many maidens, each wearing the square *coiffure*, short dress, and *petite* apron, and otherwise fully attired in the costume of the country. Each robber provided himself with a partner, and a festive dance was performed with great spirit to a popular air.

"Their gaiety was at its height, when suddenly the sound of a distant bell stole with milky gentle-

ness on the ear. In an instant all present fell on
their knees, and, with their arms devoutly crossed
upon their breasts, raised, in heavenly unison, their
hymn of votive praise to the Virgin."

Here endeth the first chapter of the " Emerald
Monster of the Deep Dell."

As "a satire on the literary absurdities of the
day," to quote its author, this capital fooling could
not be surpassed ; indeed, to those who remember,
as the present writer can distinctly, the effusions in
prose and verse—or, as Jerrold called it, " prose
and worse "—that more or less filled the pages of
the Keepsakes, the Books of Gems and Beauty of
a long bygone time, the " Monster of the Deep
Dell" is scarcely a caricature.

But I have not yet done with him. The second
chapter is devoted to an account in Grabalotti
language of the early life and loves of the interesting bandit :

" Rino Grabalotti is my name," he says. " Italy
is my nation ; the Deep Dell is my dwelling-place,
and—but no ! never shall monkish cant pollute the
lips to baleful imprecation attuned for ever. Let
the blue and hideous glare of the lightning, and
the ghastly gleam of the hag-ridden meteor, illumine
the deeds of my doing. Growl, ye thunders !

Roar, ye tempests! Yell, ye fiends, and howl in hideous harmony a prelude to my tale!"

He then proceeds to inform the artist (who, with an eye for copy, ventures to hint " that an outline of his history would be interesting ") that he was the son of a priest, and born in Naples; and naturally much annoyed by the scandalous irregularity of his birth, he devotes his life to robbing and murdering as many of his fellow-creatures as good fortune places in his hands in the practice of his profession.

But I anticipate. Grabalotti declines to say much about his infancy; he seems to have been pretty often reminded of the scandal of his birth, and as often he registered a vow that, sooner or later, he would close for ever the mouths of the slanderers.

" It was in my sixteenth summer," he continues, " that I really began to live. Though in years a boy, I was in all else a man. Passion hurtled in my darkening eye, and plunged my heart in lava. I loved; what Italian at my age does not? Yes; I—the ruthless, the scathed, the smouldering, the sanguinary, the Emerald Monster of the Deep Dell —I, even I, gasped with tortuous anguish in the maddening transports of Cupid."

Giulia is the name of the fair creature who has caused the eruption of this volcanic passion ; and on what the bandit-lover calls " an evening of rosy gladness," he seeks his fair enslaver's window, guitar in hand. But the voice, " which was the best at a barcarole of any in Naples," had raised a very few love notes, when a rough voice exclaims :

" ' What dost thou here, spurious offspring of sacrilege ?' accompanying the inquiry by an equally rough salutation from behind (oh, madness !)— ' begone !'

" Confusion simmered in my brain. Frenzied, I turned ; one stroke of my stiletto, and my wounded honour was salved—with gore. It was that of Giulia's father !"

This sudden death of the author of her being offended Giulia, and she solemnly renounced young Grabalotti for ever. This intimation, conveyed in a mixture of " indignation mingled with scorn," had an extraordinary effect. Says the lover :

" Twisting in bitterness awhile I lingered, then rushed distracted from the spot, and fled hissing with desperation to the mountains."

The beauties of the Deep Dell produced no soothing effect on the desperate bitterness that twisted the soul of Grabalotti; he issued from the Dell to "soak and steep his heart in blood."

"The dewy wail of infancy, the piercing zest of female innocence, and the tremulous pleading of piping feebleness, all mocked at the radiance of the crimson steel, have poured their bootless incense o'er my breast. . . . Ha, ha! The nun, her dove-like innocence devastated, has broiled like a chestnut amid the ashes of her convent," etc.

More "copy" in the style of the above is imparted to the artist. But an interruption takes place. A brigand enters, and so irritates the monster by the abruptness of his appearance that, had not the pistol with which his impatient master received him missed fire, his brains would have been scattered to the winds of heaven.

"'Ha! dost thou dare to break in upon my mood?' roared Grabalotti.

"'Come to tell you,' said the robber (speaking in the greatest possible haste), 'that the nun who escaped the sacking of the convent has been taken.'

"'Do as you list with her, and chop her head off! Stay, I would fain see it when it is done; and here, take this purse for the risk thou hast encountered.'"

Yet another interruption—this time in the person of a brigand spy disguised as a peasant. The chief

anticipates startling and perhaps unpleasant news,
and saying : " ' Excuse me, signor, for a few moments,' he retires with his emissary."

Grabalotti was absent some little time, during
which the artist " added another sketch to his small
collection," when the monster returned, and informed
his guest " in a lively tone" that they were about to
have " some fun."

" ' Of what description ?' inquired the artist.

" ' In an hour's time we shall be attacked by the
military,' " to whom he promises a warm reception ;
and in the event of the robbers being overpowered
by numbers, " a train communicates with the magazine below."

" Here the head of the unfortunate nun made its
appearance on a silver dish.   Its loveliness, even in
death, was intensely overpowering.   With a grin of
fiendish malice, Grabalotti seized it by the hair, but
no sooner did the features meet his eye, than he
relinquished his hold and fell, senseless, backwards,
faintly gasping, like a dying echo, ' 'Tis she!   'Tis
Giulia !!' "

Unless the artist guest was possessed of courage
uncommon among our fraternity, he could not have
contemplated being blown into the air with the
robbers, or being shot by the soldiers, with equa-

nimity ; and he must have been much relieved in
any case by Grabalotti, who, when " the violence of
frantic ferocity " had given way to " the calm pro-
fundity of despair," muttered in a low and suppressed
tone : " Nay, thou shalt live to tell the world my
story !" and to enable his guest to do this eventually,
" in a tone of sweetest melancholy " he said :

" Stranger, hence ! thy further stay is perilous.
Yon by-path will conduct thee to the valleys."

Rising from " the valleys " was a crag, to the
summit of which half an hour's walk would take
the artist, and from thence he was assured that " if
he turned his gaze backwards he should see something worth seeing."

The narrator tells us that he reached the crag in
twenty-nine minutes exactly.

" For one minute I gazed in the direction of the
Brigands' Haunt, from which, precisely at the expira-
tion of that time, a vivid flash of flame, shooting into
the air, accompanied by a dense column of smoke,
and followed by a terrific explosion, proclaimed too
plainly the last achievement of the Emerald Monster
of the Deep Dell."

Mr. Percival Leigh contributes a second story to
the " Fiddle-Faddle Fashion-book," in which the

novel of fashionable life, not uncommon fifty years
ago, is satirized under the title of " Belleville : a
Tale of Fashionable Life," not less happily than the
sanguinary and terribly romantic writers are treated
in the burlesque of Grabalotti.   The " Clara Matilda
poets" of the Keepsake time are also amusingly
parodied in some short poems, which, with comic ad-
vertisements, occasionally very humorous, fill up the
literary portion of the " Fiddle-Faddle Fashion-book."

   This book is not the only one in which Leech's
powers have been enlisted—I was nearly saying
prostituted—in publications devoted to eccentricities
in dress and the caprices of fashion.   In illustrations
by him of the tale of fashionable life, or of Grabalotti, the genius of that great artist would have had
full play ; but as the draughtsman of fashion-plates
it was, in my opinion, degraded.   In vindication of
my judgment I present my readers with two plates
from the " Fiddle-Faddle " book, in which Leech
portrays — no doubt under direction—caprices of
fashion which could only have existed in his own
imagination, and produced with a feeling of caricature that is so conspicuous by its absence in his
usual work.

   I now return to the paper which Mr. Leigh wrote
with a view to this memoir.

That Leigh and Leech first met as students at
St. Bartholomew's Hospital, I have noted elsewhere ;

and the details of his apprenticeship to the eccentric
surgeon, which Mr. Leigh heard from Leech him-

self, I have also given, with the exception of one incident of which I was ignorant.

"In his dispensary," says Mr. Leigh, "the doctor had one drawer amongst his boxes, in which there were pills of gentle efficacy, intended to be served out (they were made, I believe, of bread and soap) to the generality of his customers. This receptacle bore the label of ' Pil. Hum.,'—abbreviation of humbug—or, as their concoctor used to call them, ' Humbugeraneous Pills.' The Dr. Cockle to whom, Mr. Leigh says, Leech went after he left Mr. Whittle, was the son of the inventor of Cockle's Pills.

"No sooner had he become of age," continues Mr. Leigh, "than he was induced, in order to meet difficulties for which he was not responsible, to accept an accommodation bill, which the drawer of, when it fell due, failed to supply the means of meeting. Leech was consequently arrested for debt at the suit of this discounter, and lodged in a sponging-house kept by a sheriff's officer, a Jew, by name (I think) of Levi, in Newman Street. There he remained about a fortnight, supporting himself in the meanwhile by drawing cartoons and caricatures. He lithographed them on stone for Spooner, in the Strand, at a guinea each, a *friend* having negotiated their sale.

"At last, an advance of money on a projected publication sufficient to discharge the debt having been obtained, he was liberated.   But not long after, a second scrape—a repetition of the first—cost him another temporary sojourn with another Jew in another sponging-house in Cursitor Street.   This detention, however, lasted but a few days.   *From that period to the close of his life* he remained subject to repeated demands for pecuniary assistance under continued pressure, which, as at the outset, he could not withstand.   The deficits he had to defray were always heavy ; the last of them, as I understand, a thousand pounds.   It cost him very hard work to make it good.   Excess of generosity was his greatest failing."

I have no means of knowing, nor do I desire to know, who the borrowers were to whom Percival Leigh alludes ; but his revelations make the fact of Leech having died a comparatively poor man comprehensible enough.   If ever man was killed by overwork, Leech was that man, and this must be a painful reflection for those whose incessant demands upon him made it only possible for him to meet them by the incessant exertions which destroyed him.

Mr. Leigh's paper concludes with the anecdote that follows :

" Leech and Albert Smith worked together very harmoniously as illustrator and writer in several books—' Ledbury,' ' Brinvilliers,' and many others— and one day when they were leaving Smith's house together, a street - boy stepped up to them, and scoffing at the inscription on Smith's large brass door-plate, cried :

"'Oh yes ! Mr. Albert Smith, M.R.C.S., Surgeon-Dentist.'

" ' Good boy !' said Leech, putting a penny into the boy's hand ; ' now go and insult somebody else.' "

CHAPTER IV.

MR. MULREADY, R.A., was commissioned by the authorities to design a postal envelope for general use, a penny stamp affixed insuring free delivery of letters all over England. The design, which should have been of a simple character, was far too ornate and elaborate. At the top Britannia was represented in the act of despatching winged messengers with letters to all parts of the world, and down the sides of the envelope were the recipients of letters which had conveyed heart-breaking news to one side, and good tidings to the other. As a work of art the Mulready envelope has, in my opinion, great merit, but it was ludicrously inappropriate to the purposes for which it was intended. Leech saw and seized the opportunity, with the result appended.

The signature of the bottled leech, so familiar

afterwards, is used here as Mulready's signature, and
" thereby hangs a tale," which, though the burden

of it deals with a future time, I venture to introduce
in this place.

My friend Augustus Egg, R.A., who lived in a
charming house in Queen's Road, Bayswater, was
not only well known as an excellent artist, but also
as being the Amphitryon whose hospitality was
famous, and whose dinners were still more famous
by reason of the guests who were wont to surround
his table.   Where is the hungry man who would
not have been enchanted to meet Dickens and
Leech, Mark Lemon and John Forster (Dickens's
biographer), Hawkins, Q.C. (now the judge), Landseer, Mulready, Webster, and other artists less
famous?   Of these dinners I shall have something
to say by-and-by ; at present I confine myself to one
special occasion.

It was on one day during the year 1847 that Egg
said to me :

" You know Mulready better than I do ; I wish
you would go and get him to fix a day to dine here
—any day next week will suit me.   Leech wants to
meet him ; and, somehow or other, though both have
dined here frequently, they have never met."

" Good," said I ; " I will do your bidding."

And on the following Sunday I called upon
Mulready.

" Egg will be pleased if you will dine with him any
day next week, sir, that you may be disengaged.

He expects the usual set—Dickens, Landseer,
Leech, and the rest. You have never met Leech, I
think ; he is very desirous to make your acquaintance."

" Ah, is he ? Well, I don't care about knowing
Leech."

" Really, sir " (it was always the Johnsonian *sir* to
the old gentleman), said I, when I had recovered
from my surprise, "may I ask why you won't meet
Leech ?"

" Yes, you may," said the old painter, "and I will
tell you. Of course you remember that unfortunate
postal envelope that I designed ? Well, Leech
caricatured it. You needn't look so surprised—you
don't think I am such a fool as to mind being caricatured ; but I do mind being represented as a *blood-
sucker !* What else can he mean by using that
infernal little leech in a bottle in the front of his
caricature as my signature ? You know well enough,
Frith, that I have never asked monstrous prices for
my pictures. You fellows get better paid for your
work than I ever did, and you wouldn't like to be
called blood-suckers, I expect."

Mr. Mulready was an Irishman, and rather a
peppery one ; and I am happy to say that I over-
came my disposition to laugh in his face mainly

through a feeling of astonishment that my old friend
could be ignorant of the ordinary way in which
Leech signed his drawings.

" Do you happen to have a number of *Punch* by
you, Mr. Mulready?" said I.

" No ; as a languid swell said when he was asked
that same question, ' I am no bookworm ; I never
see *Punch.*' "

As I could not give my angry friend ocular proof
of his mistake by producing the usual signature to
Punch drawings, I set to work to explain how the
little leech came into the bottle, and, without much
difficulty, convinced my old friend that an insult to
him was not intended.

The two artists met; and it was delightful to
watch Leech's handsome face as Mulready himself
told of his misconception.   First there was a serious,
almost pained, expression, which, no doubt, arose in
that tender heart from being the innocent cause of
pain to another ; the serious look passed off, to give
place to a smile, which broadened into a roar of
laughter.   From that moment Leech and Mulready
were fast friends.

With an apology for the interruption, I return to
my narrative.

Alas ! I can well remember the appearance of the

" Sketches by Boz," to be so quickly followed by the
" Posthumous Papers of the Pickwick Club."   None
but those who witnessed it can conceive the enthusiasm with which that immortal work was received
by an eager public, who welcomed each number as
it appeared, month after month, with hearty appre-
ciation.   Of course, there were carping critics, one
of whom is reported to have said the author would
" go up like a rocket and come down like a stick."
That prophet, a man of much literary ability, drank
himself into a debtors' prison, where, I was told, he
died of delirium tremens.

There is, I think, a vein of melancholy unusually
developed in the nature of almost all humorists.
As an instance, I may give the actor Liston, whose
humour on the stage was to me unparalleled ; off it,
he was gloom personified.   Gillray, the caricaturist,
died melancholy mad ; and poor Seymour, the first
illustrator of " Pickwick," committed suicide.   I may
remark in this place the surprise with which I heard
Leech say that he could see no fun in any of Seymour's sketches.

In a walk that we took together, I tried to con-
vert him by naming several examples of what appeared to me humorous work.

" No," said Leech ; " the only drawing I ever saw

by Seymour that appeared funny to me was one
in which two cockneys were represented out shooting. They are about to load their guns, when one
says to the other :

"'I say, which do you put in first—powder or
shot ?'

"'Why, powder, to be sure,' said his friend.

"'Do you ?' was the reply. 'Then I don't!'"

I can vividly recall the shock occasioned by
Seymour's death. He was fairly prosperous, I
believe. His engagement to illustrate "Pickwick"
was a lucrative one, and he was much employed in
other work. In spite of all these advantages, the
humorist's melancholy was fatal to him.

I was present at the banquet at the Royal
Academy when Thackeray, in returning thanks for
literature—Dickens being present—told us how,
on finding there was a vacancy for an illustrator of
"Pickwick," he took a parcel of drawings to the
author and applied for the place. From my own
knowledge of Thackeray's limited powers as an
artist, I should have been sure of the failure of his
application. Very different would have been the
fate of Leech, who was also anxious to supply
Seymour's place ; but he was too late, for Dickens
had already chosen Hablot K. Browne, who, under

the sobriquet of " Phiz," worked in harmony with his author for very many years. There was no doubt a disposition on the part of " Phiz" to exaggeration in his illustration of Dickens' characters (already fully charged, so to speak, by their author), sometimes to the verge of caricature, and even beyond it ; this fault Leech would have avoided, as his exquisite etchings in Dickens' Christmas books fully prove.

CHAPTER V.

"THE PHYSIOLOGY OF EVENING PARTIES,"
BY ALBERT SMITH.

I HAVE already spoken of the extreme difficulty
of collecting material for this book, and to difficulty
must be added the expense which is incurred by
my publisher. I bear the latter affliction with the
equanimity common to those who escape it ; indeed,
there is a kind of satisfaction in finding that books
which are perfectly worthless as literary productions
are so highly valued on account of the prints which
illustrate them. I venture to give an instance in a
very little book called " The Physiology of Evening
Parties," written by Albert Smith. My reader will
be able to judge by the extracts given in explanation of the drawings, of the merits of Mr. Smith's
part in the " Physiology." This work, published at
2s. 6d. when clean and new, costs 18s. 6d. when
well " worn on the edge of time," yellow, dirty, and

unbound. The "Physiology" first saw the light
in 1840. I plead again for forgiveness for chronological shortcomings, which my difficulties make
unavoidable.

My first illustration represents a mamma and her
two daughters in the serious business of selecting
guests for an evening party.

"It is evening," says Mr. Albert Smith;
"mamma and her two daughters are seated at a
table arranging the names of the visitors upon the
back of an old letter, having turned out the dusty
record of the card-basket before them in order that
no one of importance may be forgotten.

"ELLEN (*loc.*): 'I am sure I don't see why we
should invite the Harveys, mamma. They have
been here twice, and never asked us back again.'

"FANNY: 'And we shall see those dreadful silver
poplins again; they must be intimately acquainted
with the cane-work of all the rout-seats in London.'

"ELLEN: 'And William Harvey is so exceedingly
disagreeable; he always looks at the ciphers on the
plate to see if it is borrowed or not.'

"FANNY: 'And last year he declared the pine-
apple ice was full of little square pieces of raw
potato; and when Mr. Edwards broke a tumbler
at supper he told him "not to mind, for they were

only tenpence apiece in Tottenham Court Road."
The low wretch! he thought he had made a capital
joke.'

"MAMMA: 'Well, my dears, I think your papa
will be annoyed if they are left out; but never mind
him—we won't ask them.'"

The discussion respecting the guests goes on,

"MAMMA AND THE GIRLS."

opinion as to eligibility widely differing.   Mamma
proposes Mr. and Mrs. Howard and the four girls,
to which Miss Ellen says:

"All dressed alike, and standing up in every
quadrille.   I declare I will get George Conway to
put an ice in Harriet's chair for her to sit down
upon, in revenge for her waltzing last year, when

she brushed down the Joan of Arc, and knocked its head off."

This refined conversation continues till Miss Ellen speaks of her brother's disposition to interfere with the invitation-list ; she says :

"'We must tell Tom not to overdo us so much with his own friends. I declare last year I did not

"Two Rude Young Men."

know half the young men in the room ; and it was so very awkward when you had to introduce them."

"Fanny : 'And they were not nice persons. Two of them were in the pit of the Lyceum the next night, and, seeing us in Mr. Arnold's box, would stare us out of countenance. With a single glass, too !'"

" And in this style," says our author, "the list
is arranged, the hostess gradually becoming a prey
to isinglass and acute mental inquietude, which
gradually increases as the day draws nearer, until
upon the morning of its arrival her very brain is

"THE HEAD OF THE HOUSE."

almost turned to blancmange from the intensity of
her anxiety !"

The whole house is, of course, turned topsy-
turvy ; and Leech gives us a picture of the master
of the mansion surrounded by some of the consequences of giving an evening party.

"This state of things," says the chronicler,

"much delights the olive-branches of the family, who, left entirely alone, and quite overlooked in the general *mêlée*, divert themselves by poking their little puddy fingers into the creams, and scooping out the insides of divers patties with a doll's leg," etc., etc.

"AN OLIVE-BRANCH."

The ball begins under sundry difficulties. A most desirable person, "*one* for whom the party was almost given, sends a melancholy statement of the very acute attack of influenza under which *they* are labouring," which they extremely regret will prevent their accepting, etc. Then one of the intended *belles* of the evening is obliged to go suddenly into the country, to see a sick aunt, but "she sends her two brothers—tall, *gangling*, awkward young men who wear pumps and long black stocks, and throw

their legs about when they are dancing everywhere
but over their shoulders," etc., etc., says the author.
Here is what Leech thinks of the two brothers.

I have never met with the word "gangling"

"Two 'Gangling' Young Men."

before; is it an invention of Mr. Albert Smith's?
I can speak to the truth of the dress of these long
brothers, for I who write have worn the long black
stock and the peculiarly cut coat and waistcoats at
many an evening party.

The numerous illustrations of " The Physiology "
are such perfect examples of Leech's earlier work,
and in themselves so good, that I am induced to
produce several more of them. I don't know whether
the fascinating person under the hands of the hairdresser is Miss Ellen or Miss Fanny. I confess
I can scarcely believe she would talk like either of

" PREPARING FOR THE BALL."

them ; happy barber ! perfect you are as you ply
your vocation ; and in that vocation—insomuch as
you have that sweet creature to contemplate—to be
envied indeed !

Then we have the greengrocer, " who is to
assist in waiting. . . . He wears white cotton
gloves with very long fingers, and was never known
to announce a name correctly, so the astonished

visitor is ushered into the room under any other
appellation than his own."

"THE ASSISTANT-WAITER."

"THE BAND."

The band must not be forgotten. " The music
arrives," says the writer, " sometimes in the shape of

a single pianist of untiring fingers and unclosing eyes ; sometimes as a harp, piano, and cornopean, who are immediately installed in a corner of the room with two chairs, a music-stool, and a bottle of marsala."

I ask my reader to note the individuality in the four faces in this drawing—and in the figures no less than in the heads—each a strongly-marked personality precisely appropriate to the instrument upon which he performs. How admirable is the cornet-a-piston gentleman contrasted with the pianoforte player !

The mistress of the house is described as making "uphill attempts at conversation" pending the arrival of a sufficient number of guests to make up a quadrille. Two old ladies, however, have already put in an appearance, and have taken possession of the best seats to "see the dancing," from which all attempts to move them to the card-room are successfully resisted. There they sit, poor old wallflowers ! with all the advantage that " false hair and turbans " can give them. Though the execution of this drawing lacks the perfection of workmanship of Leech's later manner, he never surpassed it in expression and character.

The music "strikes up," the lady of the house

throws a comprehensive *coup d'œil* over her assembled
visitors, and at last pitches upon a tall young man—
whom some of you may have met before—with short
hair, spectacles, and turned-up wristbands, as if he
was about to wash his hands with his coat on.   His

" WALLFLOWERS."

fate is sealed, and she advances towards him, blandly
exclaiming :

" *Mr. Ledbury*, allow me to introduce you to a
partner."

My own readers have heard of Mr. Ledbury ;
but as I think they are unacquainted with his per-

sonal appearance, I propose to introduce him to them, and here he is—

"MR. LEDBURY."

Mr. Ledbury is "presented to a bouquet with a young lady attached to it"—a Miss Hamilton—who freezes him completely. A quadrille is formed. Mr. Ledbury cudgels his brains for five minutes. The young partner seems to be "searching after some imaginary object amongst the petals of her bouquet." The mountainous Ledbury brain is in labour. Behold the production!

"MR. L. 'Have you been to many parties this season?'

"MISS H. 'Not a great many.'

Miss Hamilton continues the bouquet investigation. The gentleman invents another sentence.

"Mr. L. 'What do you think of Alfred Tennyson?'

"Miss H. 'I am sorry to say I have not heard his poetry. Have you?'

"Mr. Ledbury and Miss Hamilton."

"Mr. L. 'Oh yes! several times.'

Mr. Ledbury waits to be asked about "Mariana" and "Locksley Hall." No inquiry, so he "rubs up an idea upon another tack":

"Mr. L. 'What do you think of our *vis-à-vis?*'

"Miss H. 'Which one?'

"Mr. L. 'The lady with that strange head-dress. Do you know her?'

"Miss H. 'It is Miss Brown—my cousin.'"

Mr. Ledbury wishes he could fall through a trap in the floor.

The quadrille continues, with occasional attempts on the part of the brilliant couple to make conversation. The acme of imbecility seems to be reached when the lady asks if Mr. L. plays any instrument? He replies that he plays the flute a little. Does she admire it?

"Oh, so very much!" she says.

A waltz is proposed, but that form of dancing is, says our author, "never established without a prolonged desire on the part of everybody to relinquish the honour of commencing it. At last the example is set by one daring pair, timidly followed by another couple, and then by another, who get out of step at the end of the first round, and after treading severely upon the advanced toes of the old lady in a very flowery cap and plum-coloured satin (one of our faded wallflowers), who is sitting out at the top of the room, and who from that instant deprecates waltzing as an amusement not at all consistent with her ideas of feminine decorum."

The young lady in this drawing has much of

Leech's charm ; but I should scarcely have selected
it were it not for the figure of the gentleman, which
exactly resembles that of Leech himself as I first
knew him.   If conservatories, or even staircases,

"THE WALTZ."

could speak, what flirtations they could chronicle,
what love-tales they could tell!   Mr. Smith says
"you will have to confess your inability to imagine
what on earth the gentleman with the long hair, who

is carefully balancing himself on one leg against the flowerpot-stand, and the pretty girl with the bouquet, can find to talk about so long, so earnestly."

I for one beg Mr. Albert Smith's pardon. I can easily imagine what they are talking about.

"In the Conservatory."

It would be a grave omission if " The Belle of the Evening " were left out of these extracts from the " Physiology of Evening Parties." Let me present her, then. Now listen to the flourish with which the author introduces her :

"Room for beauty! The belle of the evening claims our next attention, the lovely dark-eyed girl so plainly yet so elegantly dressed, who wears her hair in simple bands over her fair forehead, un-encumbered by flower or ornament of any kind, and moves in the light of her own beauty as the presid-

"THE BELLE OF THE EVENING."

ing goddess of the room, imparting fragrance to the enamoured air that plays around her!"

Rather tall talk, this, but excusable, perhaps, as applied to the lovely creature Leech has drawn for us.

I feel I cannot close these extracts more appropri-

ately than by allowing Mr. Ledbury to appear again
at the moment of his departure from a scene in
which he has so distinguished himself by his con-
versational, as well as by his terpsichorean, powers.
He was destined to be guilty of one more folly—
that of thinking he had but to ask for his hat to
get it.

"He walks downstairs," says Mr. Smith, "under

"MR. LEDBURY'S HAT."

the insane expectation of finding his own hat, or
madly deeming that the ticket pinned upon it corre-
sponds with the one in his waistcoat pocket."

Here I take my leave of "The Physiology of
Evening Parties" in presenting my reader with this
charming little drawing, in which one scarcely knows
which to admire most—the bewildered expression of

Mr. Ledbury as he ruefully contemplates the rim of
his hat, or the sympathetic, half-laughing face of the
perfect little maid.   The artistic qualities of this
illustration are excellent.   I say good - bye to
" Evening Parties " only to meet Mr. Albert Smith
again in a work by him called " Comic Tales and
Pictures of Life," published, I think, about the time
of the " Evening Parties," or perhaps earlier, for the
illustrations are, on the whole, inferior to those in the
latter production.   The work under notice is composed of a series of short stories, in which love,
comedy, and deep tragedy play alternate parts.
Leech's attention is mainly devoted to the comic
scenes.

We are told of a Mr. Percival Jenks, whose
frequent visits to the theatre have led to the loss
of his heart to a beauteous ballet-girl.   " The third
ballet-girl from the left-hand stage-box, with the
golden belt and green wreath, in the Pas des Guir-
landes, or lyres, or umbrellas, or something of the
kind, had enslaved his susceptible affections."

No one knew who Mr. Jenks was, or what he
was.   Even his landlady's information about him
was confined to the idea that he was " something in
a house in the City."   That idea proved to be well
founded, for Mr. J. was discovered by the head-clerk

at the house in the City, spoiling blotting-paper by
drawing little opera-dancers all over it; thus neglecting his accounts, which he had to "stay two
hours after time to make up.   At half price, nevertheless, he was at the play again, his whole existence
centred on an airy compound of clear muslin and

"MR. PERCIVAL JENKS."

white satin that was twirling about the stage."
Mr. Jenks burned to know his enslaver's name
with a view to an introduction; and for that purpose
he haunted the stage-door, but utterly failed to
recognise, amongst the faded cloaks, and drabby

bonnets that issued from that portal, the angelic
form of his charmer.   He then took to haunting
the places where minor actors and other employés
of the theatre most do congregate for the purpose of
social intercourse and refreshment ; here at last he is
rewarded.

"Do you know the young lady," he says to a
habitué, "who dances in the ballet with a green
wreath round her head ?"

"And a gilt belt round her waist ?" asked the
friend in turn.   "Oh, it's Miss—Miss—I shall forget my own name next."

Percival was about to suggest Rosière, Céleste,
Amadée, and other pretty cognomens, when his
companion caught the name, and exclaimed :

"Miss Jukes ; I thought I should recollect
it."

The name certainly was not what Percival had
expected ; still, what was in a name ? Jenks was
not poetical, and Jukes was something like it.

"Could you favour me with an introduction to
her ?" he asked.

"In a minute, if you wish it," replied his companion.

"You know her intimately then ?"

"Very ; I buy all my green-grocery of her."

The introduction takes place. Gracious powers! how a minute broke the enchantment of many weeks! "The nymph of the Danube was habited in a faded green cloak and straw bonnet, with limp and half-bleached pink ribbons clinging to its form. Her pallid and almost doughy face was deeply pitted with smallpox; her skin was rough from the constant layers of red and white paint it had to endure," etc., etc. He fell back with a convulsive start.

From internal evidence I find the date of "Comic Tales," etc., to be 1841, contemporary, therefore, with the establishment of *Punch*. There is a drawing of so pretty a conceit as to warrant my selecting it, though artistically it is inferior to Leech's work even at that time. The drawing heads a paper entitled "Speculations on Marriage and Young Ladies," and as it tells its own story, quotation from Mr. Smith is needless.

In one amusing paper in "Comic Tales," the author treats us to "an Act for amending the representation of certain public sights, termed equestrian spectacles, in the habit of being represented at a favourite place of resort, termed the Royal Amphitheatre, Westminster Bridge." The paper is framed in the form of an Act of Parliament, and the author forbids the use of ancient jokes or stereotyped phrases in a very humorous manner.

"Be it enacted," he announces, after condemning a variety of objectionable practices, "that the clown shall not, after the first equestrian feat, exclaim: 'Now I'll have a turn to myself!' previous to his toppling like a coach-wheel round the ring; nor shall he fall flat on his face, and then collecting some sawdust in his hand, drop it down from the level of his head, and say his nose bleeds; nor shall he attempt to make the rope-dancers' balance-pole stand on its end by propping it up with the said sawdust; nor shall he, after chalking the performers' shoes, conclude by chalking his own nose, to prevent his foot slipping when he treads upon it; nor shall he pick up a small piece of straw, for fear he should fall over it, and afterwards balance the said straw on his chin as he runs about; neither shall the master of the ring say to the clown, when they are leaving the circus: 'I never follow the fool, sir!' nor shall the fool reply: 'Then I do!' and walk out after him."

I would draw attention to the figure of the clown in this cut, which is simply perfect in expression and character. The affected strut of the ring-master also is admirably caught.

A paper on Christmas pantomimes is illustrated

by such a perfect clown that I cannot resist my inclination to present him to my readers.

CLOWN : " Oh, see what I've found !"

" Comic Tales and Pictures of Life " contains, at least, one drawing that is equal to Leech at his best. The cut illustrates an article on " Delightful People," a short essay, amusing enough.

Music, whether performed by the band or by musical guests, is an important factor in an evening party. Mr. Albert Smith tells us that " a lady of his acquaintance" had secured those " Delightful People, the Lawsons," for a large evening party she was about to give ; and after lauding the charming qualities of Mr. and Mrs. Lawson, she put a final touch

to the Lawson attractions by informing her friend
that their daughter, Miss Cinthia Lawson, was not
only a delightful girl, but that "she sings better
than anyone you ever heard in private." In the
interval of dancing Cinthia sings.   "The young lady

"MISS CINTHIA SINGS."

now dressed in plain white robes, with her hair
smoothed very flat round her head *à la Grisi*, whom
she thought she resembled both in style of singing
and features, and consequently studied all her atti-
tudes from the clever Italian's impersonation of
Norma. . . . At last the lady begun a *bravura* upon

such a high note, and so powerful, that some impudent fellows in the square, who were passing at the
moment, sang out ' Vari-e-ty' in reply. Presently,
a young gentleman, who was standing at her side,
chanced to turn over too soon, whereupon she gave
him *such* a look, that, if he had entertained any
thoughts of proposing, would effectually have stopped
any such rash proceeding ; but her equanimity was
soon restored, and she went through the aria in
most dashing style until she came to the last note,
whose appearance she heralded with a *roulade* of
wonderful execution."

I remember Grisi, and I cannot share Miss Lawson's conviction of her resemblance to that great
singer—personal resemblance, I mean—and, in all
probability, she had as feeble a claim to an equality
of genius ; but that she had a powerful voice, and
that she gave it full effect, is evident by Leech's
perfect rendering of that wonderful mouth, from
which one can almost hear the *roulade*. All the
lines of the figure, with the movement of the hands,
and the backward action of the singer, are true to
Nature. The assistant at the music-book and the
stolid old gentleman are also excellent.

With this, the best of the drawings in "Comic
Tales," I take my leave of the book.

CHAPTER VI.

JOHN LEECH AND THE ETON BOY.

I HAD been told that a friend whose acquaintance I made many years ago was in possession of some correspondence with Leech of considerable interest. I wrote to him on the subject, and received the following reply :

" DEAR MR. FRITH,

"I had intended waiting till my return to town to see whether I could find John Leech's letters before writing to you ; but as you ask for the story, here it is, to the best of my recollection, and it is heartily at your service. When I was a boy at Eton I sent to *Punch* an incident which happened at a dance. Young Oxford complaining to his partner of the dearth of 'female society' at the University, she retorts, 'What a pity you didn't go to a girls' school instead !' Its appearance beneath an illustration of Leech's caused great excitement in our house at Eton, and as great tales of Mr. Punch's

"DREADFUL FOR YOUNG OXFORD."

LADY: "Are you at Eton?"

YOUNG OXFORD: "Aw, no! I'm at Oxford."

LADY: "Oxford! Rather a nice place, is it not?"

YOUNG OXFORD: "Hum!—haw! pretty well; but then I can't get on without female society!"

LADY: "Dear! dear! pity you don't go to a girls' school, then!"

liberality were current—as, for example, that the
sender of the advice 'To persons about to marry—
don't,' had received £100—I began to look anxiously
for some tip for my contribution.   An enterprising
pal said, 'It's a beastly shame ; and if you'll go
halves, I'll write to *Punch* and wake 'em up.'   This
speedily resulted in the receipt of a post-office order
for two guineas from John Leech, accompanied by
a rather dry note, to the effect that Mr. Punch considered that he had already done enough in providing
an original illustration to my joke.   I was indignant,
and wrote back to Leech returning the money, but
he would not hear of this.   He told me I could buy
gloves with the money for the young lady if I liked
—which I am afraid I didn't.   Several kind letters
from him followed, with an invitation, gladly accepted, to call and see him in the holidays, and a
present, which I still treasure, of two volumes of
his ' Life and Character.'

"At the time I remember my schoolfellows considered me a born caricaturist, an opinion I naturally
shared.   Leech was most indulgent to my early
efforts—gave me some wood-blocks to work upon,
and encouraged me to persevere, which, alas ! I
have not done, etc.

" Yours truly."

Here follows Leech's "dry note ":

"32, Brunswick Square, London,
"June 6, 1859.

" DEAR SIR,

"The editor of *Punch* is the person who should be addressed upon all money matters connected with that periodical. However, in the present instance, perhaps it will answer every purpose if I adopt the suggestion of your 'great *friend* and *confidant*,' and '*do the handsome* and send a *tip direct*,' which I do in the shape of a post-office order for one guinea ; or, as your 'entirely *disinterested*' young friend is to have half of what you get, it will be even better if I make the order for two guineas instead, as I do, only you must not look upon this as a precedent. I am afraid Mr. Punch would have considered that the trouble and expense he was at to have an original design made to your few lines would have been ample recompense. In future send to the editor your notion of what you expect for any contribution, and he will accept or reject accordingly, I dare say.

" Yours faithfully,
" JOHN LEECH."

The Eton boy was "indignant, and wrote back to

Leech returning the money," to which Leech replied as follows :

" 32, Brunswick Square,
"November 8, 1859.

" DEAR SIR,

"No, no; it must be as it is; besides, the order is made out in your name, and can be used by no one else.   After all, your contribution was very amusing, and pray consider yourself as quite entitled to the sum offered.   If you have any doubt as to how you should spend the money, why, then, buy some gloves for the young lady who said the smart thing to the Oxford man.   As to my being offended, dismiss the notion from your mind at once.   Your first note I consider perfectly good-natured, and your second as frank and gentleman-like.   I hope you will do me the favour to accept two volumes of my sketches, in which I hope you will find some amusement.

" I will direct the volumes to be sent to you this afternoon.

" Believe me, dear sir,
" Yours faithfully,
" JOHN LEECH."

Encouraged by Leech's kindness, and being, as he says, "a born caricaturist in the opinion of his friends," the Eton boy sent some sketches for Leech's opinion. To this application he received the following reply :

"32, Brunswick Square,
"June 11, 1859.

" MY DEAR SIR,

" I am very busy, so you must excuse a rather short note. Your sketches I have looked at carefully, however, and I have no hesitation in saying that they show a great perception of humour on your part. They seem to me to be altogether very good ; and I have no doubt that with practice you might make your talent available in *Punch* and elsewhere. I don't know about your taking lessons, except from Nature, and learn from her as much as possible. Try your hand at some initial letters—if drawn on the wood clearly, so much the better—and I will, with great pleasure, hand them to the editor of *Punch*. ' The Pleasures of Eton ' is capital ; the style, I take it, founded a little upon Doyle's works. I would not do that too much. You have quite cleverness enough to strike out a path of your own, and with my best wishes for your success,

" Believe me,

" Yours faithfully,

" JOHN LEECH."

In sending these letters the Eton boy of old says
he is "sure that nothing would more thoroughly
exemplify Leech's genial wit and courteous kindliness
than these replies to an unknown schoolboy." I
suppose the letter in which my friend was invited to
call upon Leech "in the holidays" is not to be
found. But that he did call and received a present
of "wood-blocks to work upon," accompanied by
"encouragement to persevere," which, alas! he has
not done, we have from himself.

This incident is especially delightful, as it reflects
perfectly the quality of heart and mind so characteristic of Leech.

CHAPTER VII.

MR. SPONGE'S SPORTING TOUR.

MR. SURTEES, the writer of the sporting novels, possessed considerable powers of invention, which he indulged—amongst other vagaries—in giving names to most of the characters in his books, which served to enlighten his readers as to their physical and mental peculiarities, and never more happily than when he christened the hero of this sporting tour Mr. Soapy Sponge. " Mr. Sponge," says our author, " wished to be a gentleman without knowing how ;" but what Mr. Sponge did know was how to sponge upon everybody with whom he could force an acquaintance, and this he effected with surprising success. Hunting and good hunting quarters were the objects of Mr. Sponge's machinations, and upon a half-hearted invitation from a Mr. Jawleyford, of Jawleyford Court, an invitation given without an idea that it would be accepted

(as sometimes happens), Mr. Sponge found himself
installed in the ancestral mansion of the Jawleyfords.
Mr. Jawleyford was "one of the rather numerous
race of paper-booted, pen-and-ink landowners," says
Mr. Surtees, "whose communications with his
tenantry were chiefly confined to dining with them
twice a year in the great entrance-hall after the
steward, *Mr. Screwemtight*, had eased them of their
rents. Then Mr. Jawleyford would shine forth the
very impersonification of what a landlord ought to
be. Dressed in the height of fashion, he would
declare that the only really happy moments of his
life were those when he was surrounded by his
tenantry.

In the background of this admirable drawing we
see Mr. Jawleyford's portrait, flanked by his ancestors,
on canvas and in armour, hanging on the panelled
walls of his gorgeous home. The variety of character
in the "chawbacons," each a marked individuality,
contrasts effectually with his *quasi* fashionable landlord. For the first banquet at Jawleyford Court,
"Mr. Sponge," says the author, "made himself an
uncommon swell." His dress is minutely described,
and faithfully depicted by Leech, in the etching in
which we see the sponger conducting a very portly
Mrs. Jawleyford, followed by her daughters, to the

dining-room. The young ladies who have entered the drawing-room " in the full fervour of sisterly animosity," according to the author, seem—in the lovely group that Leech makes of them—to have speedily made up their quarrel, as their entwined arms and pretty, happy faces prove. The solemn butler, who looks with awe at his aristocratic master, is in Leech's truest vein, while Mr. Jawleyford himself is simply perfect. In the footmen and page the illustration is less successful ; they seem to approach, if not to reach, caricature.

When Mr. Sponge found himself in good quarters, no hint however strong, no looks however cold, no manner however unpleasant, would move him, until he had provided himself with others to his liking. Under the impression that he was rich, the Misses Jawleyford set their caps at him. Amelia and Emily rivalled each other in tender attentions to the adventurer, who, after hesitating as to which of them he should throw the handkerchief to, fixed upon Miss Amelia, who found her sister " in the act of playing the agreeable " with Mr. Sponge as she " sailed " into the drawing-room before dinner ; then, " with a haughty sort of sneer and toss of the head to her sister, as much as to say, ' What are you doing with my man ?'—a sneer that suddenly changed into a sweet smile as her eye encountered Sponge's—she just motioned him off to a sofa, where she commenced a *sotto-voce* conversation in the engaged-couple style."

During his stay at Jawleyford Court, Mr. Sponge's time was passed in hunting, smoking all over the house—a habit the owner detested—and in making love to Miss Amelia ; taking care, however, not to commit himself until he had discovered from papa what the settlements were to be. We who are behind the scenes know that Jawleyford Court is " mortgaged up to the chimney-pots," and that Mr. J. is over head and ears in debt besides. We know also that Mr. Sponge is impecunious, his hunters are hired ; he is, in fact, as his author describes him, "a vulgar humbug." " Jawleyford began to suspect that Sponge might not be the great ' catch ' he was represented," says the author. No doubt in finding himself baffled in his attempts to sound his host upon the subject of settlements, Mr. Sponge also " began to suspect" that neither of the Misses Jawleyford would be the " catch " that he wanted. Still, he held on to his quarters in defiance of the attempts to get rid of him. He was removed from the best bedroom to one in which it was impossible to light a fire, or, rather, to endure it when it was alight, because of an incurable smoky chimney. He was given poor food and corked wine, still he stayed, until he had provided himself with a temporary home at the house of a hunting gentleman named Puffington.

Mr. Puffington, who made Sponge's acquaintance at the covert-side where Lord Scamperdale's hounds met, "got it into his head" that Mr. Sponge was a literary man, whose brilliant pen was about to be employed in the interest of fox-hunting in general, and of certain runs of Mr. Puffington's hounds in particular. Mr. Puffington "was the son of a great starch-maker at Stepney." Puffington, senior, made a large fortune, which enabled his son to become the owner of Hanby House, and of the "Mangey-sterne—now Hanby-Hounds," because he thought they would give him consequence. Our author says, Mr. Puffington "had no natural inclination for hunting," but he seems to have become M.F.H. so that he might entertain some of the sporting friends he had made at college, such "dashing young sparks as Lord Firebrand, Lord Mudlark, Lord Deuceace, Sir Harry Blueun, Lord Legbail, now Earl of Loosefish," and so on.

My space, or, rather, the want of it, prevents my telling how it was that Mr. Sponge " awoke and

found himself famous" as an author.   In conjunc-
tion with a friend, who steered him through the
spelling and grammar, he concocted an article for
the *Swillingford Patriot* — Grimes, editor — which
"appeared in the middle of the third sheet, and
was headed, 'Splendid Run with Mr. Puffington's
Hounds.'"   Mr. Grimes was ably assisted in his
editorial duties by "his eldest daughter, Lucy—a
young lady of a certain age, say liberal thirty—an
ardent Bloomer, with a considerable taste for senti-
mental poetry, with which she generally filled the
Poet's Corner."

As Mr. Puffington quite expected to be immortalized in some work of general circulation, his
indignation knew no bounds when he found himself relegated to a corner of the county paper,
and all his hopes of his doings being read by "the
Lords Loosefish, the Sir Toms and Sir Harrys of
former days" grievously disappointed.   Never,
surely, were disgust, disappointment, and rage more
perfectly expressed than in the second portrait of
Mr. Puffington : not only the face, but the whole
figure—one can fancy how the hand in the pocket
of the dressing-gown is clenched—denotes the
surprise and exasperation of the miserable man.

Mr. Sponge's literary effort has "done for him"

with Mr. Puffington. He must go. Easier said than done.

"Couldn't you manage to get him to go?" asked Mr. Puffington of his valet.

"Don't know, sir. I could try, sir—believe he's bad to move, sir," said the valet.

Driven to despair, the host "scrawled a miserable-looking note, explaining how very ill he was, how he regretted being deprived of Mr. Sponge's agreeable society—hoped he would come another time," and so on. Even the "sponger" felt the difficulty of parrying such a palpable notice to quit. "He went to bed sorely perplexed," and in his waking moments trying to remember "what sportsmen had held out the hand of good fellowship and hinted at hoping to have the pleasure of seeing him"; he could think of no one to whom he could volunteer a visit. But Fortune favours the brave sponger, as she often does unworthy people, and in Mr. Jogglebury Crowdey, an eccentric individual whose acquaintance Sponge had made in the hunting-field, he found another host. At the suggestion of Mrs. Jogglebury, who, without the slightest reason, had taken it into her head that Mr. Sponge was a wealthy man, and would make a satisfactory godfather to one of her children,

Mr. Jogglebury called on Mr. Sponge at the Puffington mansion, and invited him to " pay us a visit."

No sooner does our hero grasp the situation than he says :

" Well, you're a devilish good fellow, and I'll tell you what, as I am sure you mean what you say, I'll take you at your word and go at once."

And in this determination he persists, though Mr. J. pleads for some delay, as Mrs. Jogglebury Crowdey requires some little time for preparation in receiving so distinguished a guest.

The visit to Puddingpote Bower, as the Jogglebury dwelling was called, proved as unfortunate as the previous visits ; the more people saw of Mr. Sponge the less they liked him, and this time the dislike was mutual. " Jog and Sponge," says the author, " were soon most heartily sick of each other. Mr. Sponge soon began to think that it was not worth while staying at Puddingpote Bower for the mere sake of his keep, " seeing there was no hunting to be had from it."

Within twelve or thirteen miles from the Bower there lived Sir Harry Scattercash, a very fast young gentleman indeed. He kept " an ill - supported pack of hounds, that were not kept upon any fixed principles ; their management was only of the scrimmaging order," but Mr. Sponge, scenting an invitation, determined to make one amongst the field.

In his attempt to " go it," my lord " was ably assisted by Lady Scattercash, late the lovely and elegant Miss Glitters, of the Theatre Royal, Sadler's Wells. Lady Scattercash could ride—indeed, she used to do scenes in the circle (two horses and a flag), and she could drive, and smoke, and sing, and was possessed of many other accomplishments."

What a winning creature Leech has made of her, and the scarcely less delightful little tiger behind her, may be seen in the illustration which the law of copyright prevents me from introducing, as it also prohibits the appearance here of Sir Harry, her husband, the happy possessor of the charming Lady Scattercash.

" Sometimes," says the author of " Sponge," " Sir Harry would drink straight on end for a week!" Mr. Sponge made desperate efforts to take up his abode at Nonsuch House, but Sir Harry was surrounded by congenial spirits, who, one and all, had taken prejudice against that worthy ; so, beyond a hunting dinner, at which everybody, including the ladies, took more wine

than was good for them, Mr. Sponge and Nonsuch
House were strangers to each other for a time.
But, as the hunting-field is open to all and sundry,
Mr. Sponge, not easily daunted, put in a frequent
appearance, in the sure and certain hope that
admission to free quarters at Sir Harry's was only
delayed.   Beyond what is elegantly called " peck
and perch," Nonsuch House contained a very
powerful attraction in the form of Miss Lucy
Glitters, sister to Lady Scattercash.   Miss Lucy
was a lovely person, and her charms were increased
in Mr. Sponge's eyes because he persuaded himself
that the sister-in-law of a baronet must necessarily
be a rich woman.   Miss Lucy had also the conviction that Mr. Sponge was a rich man; how else
could he spend his time in the sports of the field,
with all their expensive accompaniments?   Miss
Glitters was a bold rider, and that accomplishment
also endeared her to the gentleman in whom the
passion of love burned suddenly, and with a very
furious flame indeed; till on one fateful hunting
day the amorous couple found themselves " in at
the death ": they had distanced the field, they were
alone.   Mr. Sponge secured the brush, and said :

"We'll put this in your hat, alongside the cock's
feathers."

I now quote my author : " The fair lady leant towards him, and as he adjusted it becomingly in her hat, looking at her bewitching eyes, her lovely face, and feeling the sweet fragrance of her breath, a something shot through Mr. Sponge's pull-devil pull-baker coat, his corduroy waistcoat, his Eureka shirt, angola vest, and penetrated to the very cockles of his heart. He gave her such a series of smacking kisses as startled her horse and astonished a poacher who happened to be hid in the adjoining hedge."

On the return of the happy pair Lucy rushes to her sister with the good news. Lady Scattercash was delighted, because " Mr. Sponge was such a nice man, *and so rich !* She was sure he was rich— couldn't hunt if he wasn't. Would advise Lucy to have a good settlement, in case he broke his neck." On further inquiry, however, her ladyship had good reason to suspect that a red coat and two or three hunters were not satisfactory proofs of wealth ; and in reply to one who knew, she retorted, " Well, never mind, if he has nothing, she has nothing, and nothing can be nicer." With the conviction that nothing could be nicer, " Lady Scattercash warmly espoused Mr. Sponge's cause," the consequence being his instalment in splendid quarters at Nonsuch

House, where he made himself thoroughly at home.
"It was very soon 'my hounds,' 'my horses,' and
'my whips,' etc., being untroubled by his total
inability to keep the angel who had ridden herself
into his affections, for he made no doubt that something would turn up." If it were not for the introduction of a delightful drawing by Leech, I should
take no note of a "Steeplechase," in which
Mr. Sponge comes before us for the last time.
This function is not a favourite with Mr. Surtees,
nor is it looked upon without much anxiety by
Miss Lucy. "She has made Mr. Sponge a white
silk jacket to ride in, and a cap of the same colour.
Altogether, he is a great swell, and very like a
bridegroom," says the author.

If this drawing suffered in the hands of the wood-
engraver, it must have been beyond imagination
beautiful, for, as it is, it shows us Leech in his full
strength.   Nothing, it seems to me, could surpass
the figure of Lucy, whose expression of loving fear
for the safety of the bold Sponge is shown to us in
one of the prettiest faces conceivable.   Sponge
himself is no less successfully rendered as he smiles
reassuringly at his beloved.   The race—admirably
described by the author—is run, and won by
Mr. Sponge.   "And now for the hero and heroine

of our tale. The Sponges—for our friend married
Lucy shortly after the steeplechase — stayed at
Nonsuch House till the bailiffs walked in. Sir
Harry then bolted to Boulogne, where he afterwards

died. Being at length starved out of Nonsuch
House," says the historian, "he—Sponge—arrived
at his old quarters, the Bantam, in Bond Street,
where he turned his attention very seriously to
providing for Lucy and the little Sponge, who had

now issued its prospectus.   He thought over all the
ways and means of making money without capital.
. . . Professional steeplechasing Lucy decried,
declaring she would rather return to her flag
exercises at Astley's as soon as she was able than
have her dear Sponge risking his neck that way.   Our
friend at length began to fear fortune-making was
not so easy as he thought ; indeed he was soon sure
of it."   Something had to be done ; "accordingly,
after due consultation with Lucy, he invested his all
in fitting up and decorating the splendid establishment in Jermyn Street, St. James's, now known as
the SPONGE CIGAR AND BETTING ROOMS, where noble-
men, gentlemen, and officers in the Household troops
may be accommodated with loans on their personal
security to any amount.   We see by Mr. Sponge's
last advertisement that he has £116,000 to lend
at 3½ per cent.

CHAPTER VIII.

"THE MARCHIONESS OF BRINVILLIERS,"
BY ALBERT SMITH.

"December 20, 1844.

"MY DEAR SIR,

"Here we are at the 20th of the month,
and I have only four pages of Smith's new story—
no incident. Really, it is too much to expect that
I can throw myself at a moment's notice into the
seventeenth century, with all its difficulties of
costume, etc., etc. What am I to do? There is a
great want of system somewhere. I received a note
from Mr. Marsh last night, stating for the first time
that there would be *two* illustrations to 'The Marchioness of Brinvilliers,' and also urging me to be
very early with the plates, it being Christmas and
all that! But, as I said before, I have not the
matter to illustrate. *What am I to do?* Added to
all this, I must be engaged one day in the early part

of next week on the melancholy occasion of the
funeral of a poor little sister of mine.   Pray, my
dear sir, do what you can to expedite matters, and

" Believe me,

" Yours faithfully,

" JOHN LEECH.

"—— MORGAN, ESQ."

The above is one of the many letters that might
be quoted to show the aggravating delays and difficulties under which so much of Leech's work was
produced.   I take Mr. Morgan to have been one of
the officials of Mr. Richard Bentley's establishment,
whose patience must have been sorely tried again
and again by the pranks of that *genus irritabile*,
the writer.   Judging from the humorous character
of Albert Smith's " Ledbury " and other works, one
is hardly prepared for the horrors that make us
shudder over the [pages of " The Marchioness of
Brinvilliers "—horrors in which the writer seems to
revel with a zest as keen as that he takes in the
fun and frolic of Ledbury.

The "shilling shocker" of the present day is a
mild production indeed, in comparison with the
history of the poisoner and adulteress, Brinvilliers,
in which "on horror's head horrors accumulate."
The authors of the modern productions are, for the

most part, inventors of the blood-and-murder scenes
that adorn their books. Not so Mr. Albert Smith,
whose pages describe but too truly the career of the
most notorious of the many criminals that flourished
in the most profligate period of French history.
Louis XIV. set an example in debauchery to his
subjects which the highest of them eagerly followed ;
but the most fearful factor of this terrible time was
poison, by which the possessors of estates who
"lagged superfluous on the scene" were made to
give place to greedy heirs ; husbands, inconveniently
in the way, were put out of it by their wives, whose
affections had been disposed of elsewhere ; state
officers, whose positions were desired by aspirants
unwilling to wait for them, were struck by sudden
and mysterious illness, speedily followed by death,
for which the faculty of the time could in no way
account.

Marie, Marchioness of Brinvilliers, lived with her
husband in the Rue des Cordeliers in Paris. The
Marquis was a man of easy morals, and the Marchioness was a woman of still easier morals, for she
had many lovers ; she also amused her leisure hours
by the study of the nature and properties of a great
variety of deadly poisons ; thinking, no doubt, as she
was of a jealous disposition, that the time might

arrive when her knowledge would be useful in
depriving her lover of the temptation which had
led him to forget his duty to her.   The Marchioness
was a very beautiful woman ; she had eyes of a
tender blue ; her complexion was of dazzling white-
ness, with cheeks of a delicate carnation ; her expression was angelic, and she wore her hair of
pale gold in bushy ringlets, in obedience to the
fashion of the time.   We first become acquainted
with the Marchioness under painful circumstances,
for she made—and kept—an appointment with one
lover without being sufficiently careful to disguise
her doings from another.   That other was the
Chevalier Gaudin de Sainte-Croix, who proceeded
to the lodgings of his rival, M. Camille Theria.

"'The Marchioness of Brinvilliers is here, I
believe,' said Gaudin to the grisette at the door.
'Will you tell her she is wanted on pressing
business ?'

"The Marchioness appeared.   A stifled scream
of fear and surprise, yet sufficiently intense to show
her emotion at the sight of Gaudin, broke from her
lips as she recognised him.   But she immediately
recovered her impassibility of features—that wonderful calmness and innocent expression which afterwards was· so severely put to the proof without

being shaken—and she asked, with apparent un-
concern :

" ' Well, monsieur, what do you want with me ?'

" ' Marie !' exclaimed Gaudin, 'let me ask your
business here at this hour' (it was rather late)
' unattended, and in the apartment of a scholar of the
Hôtel Dieu ?'

" ' You are mad, Sainte-Croix,' said the Marchioness. ' Am I to be accountable to you for all
my actions ? M. Theria is not here, and I came to
see his wife on my own affairs.'

" ' Liar !' cried Gaudin."

The lady had not told the truth, for M. Theria
had no wife, and he was so near by that he heard
the angry voice of M. Sainte-Croix, who so convinced the Marchioness of her perfidy that "in an
instant the accustomed firmness of the Marchioness
deserted her, and she fell upon her knees at his feet
on the cold, damp floor of the landing."

In this powerful etching nothing could surpass the
beauty of the face and figure of the Marchioness ;
she exactly realizes our ideal. But the Chevalier,
though full of passion, is, to my mind, verging on the
theatrical.

Finding that her entreaties to the Chevalier to
" go away " have no effect, she threatens suicide.

" There is but one resource left," she says, as she "springs up from her position of supplication."

"Where are you going?" asked Sainte-Croix, as she rushed to the top of the flight of stairs.

" Hinder me not !" returned Marie. " To the river !"

But before she could reach the river—to which she would no doubt have given a very wide berth— she fainted, or pretended to faint, in the courtyard at the bottom of the staircase. Here the pair were overtaken by M. Theria.

" A few hot and hurried words passed on either side, and the next instant their swords were drawn and crossed. The fight was short, and ended in Sainte-Croix thrusting his rapier completely through the fleshy part of the sword-arm of the student, whose weapon fell to the ground.

" ' I have it !' cried Camille. ' A peace, monsieur ! I have it !' he continued, smiling, as he felt that his wound, though slight, was too serious to have been received in so unworthy a cause.

" As he was speaking, Marie opened her eyes and looked around. But the instant she saw the two rivals, she shuddered convulsively, and again relapsed into insensibility.

" 'She is a clever actress,' continued Camille, smiling.

" 'We have each been duped,' answered Gaudin.

" 'She will play me no longer. As far as I am concerned,' said Theria, 'you are welcome to all her affections, and I shall reckon you as one of my best friends for your visit this evening.' "

The visit was destined to have an unexpected end, however, for the attention of the Guet Royal, or night-guard, had been called to the clashing of swords.

" Some young men, who had come up with the guard as they were returning from their orgies, pressed forward with curiosity to ascertain the cause of the tumult. But from one of them a fearful cry of surprise was heard as he recognised the persons before him. Sainte-Croix raised his eyes, and found himself face to face with Antoine, Marquis of Brinvilliers !"

The late combatants threw dust in the eyes of the lady's husband cleverly enough by pretending that Sainte-Croix had rescued her from the unwelcome attentions of Theria, who had mistaken her in the uncertain light for a lady with whom he had an appointment. The cloak which the Marchioness wore, together with the darkness of the night, had

prevented his discovering that she was not the
person he expected until her cries had brought in
Sainte-Croix, who was passing, as he said himself,
" to his lodgings in the Rue des Bernardins."

The lady went home with her husband, and
Sainte-Croix retired to his lodgings, there to medi-
tate on the perfidy of his mistress. The Chevalier
de Sainte-Croix was even more learned in poisons,
and less scrupulous in the use of them, than his
mistress; and in his first gusts of passion, on discovering her treachery, he was inclined—in the hate
of her that took temporary possession of him—to
subject her to their effect; but reflection produced
demoniacal results. She should be spared to kill
those who ought to be near and dear to her!

" ' I will be her bane—her curse !' he exclaimed.
' I will be her bad angel ! . . . And I will triumph
over that besotted fool, her husband,' etc.

" He opened a small, iron-clamped box, and
brought from it a small packet, carefully sealed, and
a phial of clear, colourless fluid.

" ' I have it ! It is here—the source, not of life,
but of death !'

" Almost as he speaks, he is summoned by the
femme de chambre of the Marchioness to an interview at her residence at her father's house, the

Hôtel d'Aubray. The Chevalier found the en-
chantress in studied disarray. She might have
been made up after one of Guido's Magdalens,"
says the author, "so beautiful were her rounded
shoulders, so dishevelled her light hair," etc.

The lovers were speedily reconciled, but the lady
had an important communication to make—no less
than the discovery of their intimacy by her husband,
whom she felt sure had revealed the fact to her
father, M. d'Aubray. A long pause, broken by
Sainte-Croix :

"'Marie,' he said, 'they must die, or our happiness is impossible.'"

The Marchioness was not yet hardened enough
to receive this announcement with equanimity ; and
the lovers were still discussing the *pros* and *cons* of
it, when they were surprised by Monsieur d'Aubray,
who, entering by a secret door, "stood looking on
the scene before him." Any doubts of guilty
intimacy, if he had any, were dispelled ; and, after
ordering his daughter to her chamber, he turned to
Sainte-Croix, and said :

"'Monsieur de Sainte-Croix, I will provide you
with a lodging where you will run no risk of com-
promising the honour of a noble family.'"

And so saying, he produced a *lettre de cachet*.

armed with which the exempts, who were waiting for him, speedily deposited M. de Sainte-Croix at the Bastille. The Marchioness, separated from her children and her husband, was exiled to Offremont, a family place some distance from Paris. Here she lived with her father, who so entirely believed in her repentance and determination to lead a new life that he proposed a speedy return to Paris.

"'I have no wish to go, *mon père*,' replied the hypocrite ; 'I would sooner remain here with you— for ever !'"

After much talk and reiterated professions of sorrow for the past, the Marchioness says, in reply to her father's order that "she shall never speak to Sainte-Croix—who had been released from the Bastille—or recognise him again :

"'You shall be obeyed, monsieur—too willingly.'"

The words had not long left her lips when she placed a lamp in the window of the room, to guide her lover to a prearranged assignation.

The awful interview that followed is described in Mr. Smith's book.

The greater villain ran the risk of interruption in his lengthened arguments in favour of parricide ; but hearing approaching footsteps, Sainte-Croix hurried away.

M. d'Aubray had gone to bed. A servant suggested the night-drink.

"'I will give it to him myself, Jervais,' said the Marchioness."

Taking a jug from the man, she poured the contents into an old cup of thin silver; then, "with a hurried glance round the room, she broke the seals of the packet Sainte-Croix had left in her hands, and shook a few grains of its contents into the beverage. No change was visible; a few bubbles rose and broke upon the surface, but this was all."

Sleep had surprised M. d'Aubray. His daughter touched him lightly, and he "awoke with the exclamation of surprise attendant upon being suddenly disturbed from sleep.

"'I have brought your wine, *mon père*,' said the murderess.

"'Thanks, thanks, my good girl,' said the old man, as he raised himself up in bed, and took the cup from the Marchioness. He drank off the contents, and then, once more bestowing a benediction upon his daughter, turned again to his pillow."

Let those who desire to see how beauty can be retained, though disfigured by devilish passion, study the face of the Marchioness in this drawing.

For skilful arrangement of light and shade, and of
the objects that go to make up the *mise en scène*,
and for natural action in the figures; this drawing
takes the lead of all the admirable illustrations in
the " Marchioness of Brinvilliers."

CHAPTER IX.

"THE MARCHIONESS OF BRINVILLIERS" (*continued*).

A GREAT reception was given at Versailles by the King. M. d'Aubray was "suffering from a sudden and fearful indisposition, but he insisted upon his daughter accepting an invitation, were it only to establish her *entrée* into society."

There, amongst the trees in the gardens, the Marchioness encounters Sainte-Croix. "His face looked ghastly in the moonbeams, and his eyes gleamed with a light that conscience made demoniac in the eyes of the Marchioness."

"'You here!' she exclaimed.

"'Where should I be but in the place of rejoicing just now?' replied Gaudin through his set teeth, and with a sardonic smile. 'I am this moment from Paris. We are free!'

"'My father?' cried the Marchioness, as a terrible expression overspread her countenance.

"'He is dead,' returned Sainte-Croix, 'and we are free!'"

There was a pause, and they looked at each other for nearly a minute.

"'Come,' at length said the Marchioness, 'come to the ball.'"

A prominent and very interesting figure in Mr. Smith's book is Louise Gauthier, a girl of comparatively humble birth, who had the misfortune to love Sainte-Croix with the intense self-sacrificing love that good women so often show for bad men, who return their affection with coldness and neglect. This girl, who had become the friend of Marotte Dupré, one of the actresses in the plays of Molière which were part of the attraction at the Versailles fête, accompanied the actress to Versailles, where she accidentally overheard a conversation between the Marchioness of Brinvilliers and M. de Sainte-Croix, which not only convinced her that the love for her that Sainte-Croix had once professed was given to another, but that some fearful tie existed between the two, caused by actions which had destroyed their happiness here and their hopes of it hereafter.

She came from her concealment, and was received with jealous fury by the Marchioness, who

believed, or affected to believe, that the girl was
at "the grotto" by appointment with Sainte-
Croix. She bestowed what is commonly called "a
piece of her mind" upon her lover, and concluded
her rhapsody by informing him that from henceforth
"we meet no more." Louise, however, convinced
the passionate Marchioness that she had made no
appointment, but was at "the grotto" by, "perhaps,
a dispensation of Providence, in order that she
might, having overheard their guilty conversation,
so act upon their consciences as to "save them
both."

The first result of her good intentions is a declar-
ation to the Marchioness by Sainte-Croix that,
though there had been some love-passages between
him and the girl, they were "madness, infatuation—
call it what name you will ; but you are the only one
I ever loved." Thus the ruffian speaks in the
presence of the woman he had betrayed ; but her
love, though crushed, still urges her to become the
man's good angel, and, seizing his arm, she cries :

"'Hear me, Gaudin. By the recollection of what
we once were to each other—although you scorn me
now, and the shadowy remembrance of old times—
before these terrible circumstances, whatever they
may be, had thus turned your heart from me and

from your God, there is still time to make amends
for all that has occurred.   I do not speak for myself,
for all those feelings have passed, but for you alone.
Repent and be happy, for happy now you are not!'"

"Gaudin made no reply, but his bosom heaved
rapidly, betraying his emotion.

"'This is idle talk,' said the Marchioness. . . .
'Will you not come with me, Gaudin?'

"'Marie!' cried Gaudin faintly, 'take me where
you list.   In life or after it, on earth or in hell, I am
yours—yours only!'

"A flush of triumph passed over her face as she
led Sainte-Croix from the grotto," etc.

By the death of her father the Marchioness hoped,
not only to have freed herself and her lover from an
ever-recurring obstacle to their intercourse, but also
to have inherited a much-needed sum of money—no
less than "one hundred and fifty thousand livres
were to have been the legacy to his daughter,
Madame de Brinvilliers—and, what was more, her
absolute freedom to act as she pleased.   The money
had passed to her brothers, in trust for her, and she
was left entirely under their surveillance.

"'This must be altered,' said the Chevalier Sainte-
Croix in an interview with the *alter ego* of an Italian
vendor of poisons named Exili.'"

This man undertakes the "alteration," or, in other words, the murder, of the two brothers for a "consideration" in the form of "one-fifth of whatever may fall to the Marchioness thereupon.

"'Of course, there is a barrier between the brothers of Madame de Brinvilliers and myself,' said Sainte-Croix to his accomplice, 'that must for ever prevent our meeting. I will provide the means, and you their application.'"

Sainte-Croix had the right to claim the merit of this scheme for enriching the Marchioness, and at the same time relieving her from a guardianship that was impenetrable by her lover. The murder of her brothers seemed a trifling affair after the poisoning of her father, and she readily consented to assist in procuring a situation for the poisoner's assistant—a man named Lechaussée—in the household of her brothers, who happened, very fortunately, to be in want of a servant at the moment. How this wretch administered the poison to the two brothers, who died instantly from its effect, the curious reader may ascertain—together with the other dramatic particulars—by consulting Mr. Albert Smith's book, in which the incidents are told with great force and skill.

By eavesdropping in somewhat improbable places

—notably at a grand fête at the Hôtel de Cluny, given by the Marquis de Lauzan, the Italian poisoner Exili becomes master of the guilty pair's secrets. The Marchioness's jealousy had been aroused during the evening by Sainte-Croix's attention to an actress ; and she left the great *salon*, and retired with her friend to a cabinet, in which, after the usual denial and reconciliation, secure, as they thought, from interruption, they discussed their demoniacal schemes. As they were about to pass from the room, "a portion of a large bookcase, masking a door, was thrown open, and Exili stood before them.

The somewhat theatrical character that Leech gives to the figure of Sainte-Croix is much less apparent in this powerful drawing ; and in the figures of Exili and the Marchioness there is not a trace of it. Though the Brinvilliers is masked according to a habit of the time, we feel that the mask conceals a beautiful face, distorted by fear, no doubt, but still lovely. The Italian is altogether excellent.

Exili loses no time in turning his information to account, and in reply to Sainte-Croix, who asks him what he wants, he replies that his trade as a sorcerer is failing, and as a poisoner he is in "a yet worse position, thanks to the Lieutenant of Police, M. de la Regnie.

" 'I must have money,' he adds, 'to enable me to retire and die elsewhere than on the Grève.' "

He ends by extorting from Sainte-Croix an undertaking to share with him the wealth obtained through the murder of the brothers. But if Exili relied upon the bond as a security of value, he displayed a degree of ignorance of the human nature of such individuals as Sainte-Croix that was surprising in so astute a person.

" To elude the payment of Exili's bond," says the author, "he had determined upon destroying him, running the risk of whatever might happen subsequently through the physician's knowledge of the murders." And he had, therefore, ordered a body of the " Guard Royal to attend, when they would receive sufficient proof of the trade Exili was driving in his capacity of alchemist."

Sainte-Croix visited the Italian with excuses for the non-payment of the money early in the evening of the day on which the arrest was planned to take place later. To those excuses the poisoner listened angrily ; he discovered some valuable jewels which Sainte-Croix wore. He had purposely brushed his hand against Sainte-Croix's cloak, and in the pocket of it he felt some weighty substance. The chink assured him it was gold.

" ' You cannot have that,' said Gaudin confusedly ;
' it is going with me to the gaming-table to-night.'

" ' You have rich jewels, too, about you,' continued Exili, peering at him with a fearful expression.
' The carcanet becomes you well.   That diamond
clasp is a fortune in itself.'

" ' Not one of them is mine,' said Sainte-Croix.
' They belong to the Marchioness of Brinvilliers.' "

The Italian affected to be satisfied with the assur-
ance that the money should be paid next day, and
Sainte-Croix's doom was sealed.   The alchemist
" turned to the furnace to superintend the progress
of some preparation that was evaporating over the
fire.

" ' What have you there ?' asked Gaudin, who was
anxious to prolong the interview till the guard could
arrive.

" ' A venom more deadly than any we have yet
known—that will kill like lightning, and leave no
trace of its presence to the most subtle tests.'

" ' You will give me the secret ?' asked Gaudin.

" ' As soon as it is finished, and the time is coming
on apace.   You have arrived opportunely to assist
me.'

" He took a mask with glass eyes, and tied it
round his face.

" 'If you would see the preparation completed, you must wear one as well.'

" Exili took another visor, and, under pretence of rearranging the string, he broke it from the mask ; and then, fixing it back with some resinous compound that would be melted by the heat of the furnace, he cautiously fixed it to Sainte-Croix's face.

" 'I will mind the furnace whilst you go,' said Gaudin, in reply to the alchemist, who said he must fetch some drugs required for further operations.

" At that moment Sainte-Croix heard an adjacent bell sound the hour at which he had appointed the guard to arrive.

" 'There is no danger in this mask, you say ?'

" 'None,' said Exili.

" Anxious to become acquainted with the new poison, and in the hope that as soon as he had acquired the secret of its manufacture the guard would arrive, Gaudin bent over the furnace. Exili had left the apartment, but as soon as his footfall was beyond Sainte-Croix's hearing he returned, treading as stealthily as a tiger, and took up his place at the door to watch his prey. As Gaudin bent his head to watch the preparation more closely, the heat of the furnace melted the resin with which

the string had been fastened.   It gave way, and the
mask fell on the floor, whilst the vapour of the
poison rose full in his face almost before, in his
eager attention, he was aware of the accident.

" One terrible scream—a cry which, once heard,
could never be forgotten—not that of agony, or
terror, or surprise, but a shrill and violent indrawing
of the breath, resembling rather the screech of some
huge, hoarse bird of prey irritated to madness, than
the sound of a human voice—broke from Gaudin's
lips. Every muscle of his face was contorted into the
most frightful form ; he remained a second, and
no more, wavering at the side of the furnace, and
then fell heavily on the floor.   He was dead."

This terrible death-scene has found a perfect illustrator in John Leech. How admirable is the fiendish
expression of the poisoner as he gloats over the body
of his victim, which is drawn with a power and
truthfulness altogether perfect!   Every detail of
the laboratory how skilfully introduced, how effec-
tively rendered !

The alchemist behaved on the occasion as might
be expected.

" He darted at the dead body like a beast of prey ;
and drew forth the bag of money, which he trans-
ferred to his own pouch. He next tore away every

ornament of any value that adorned Gaudin's costly
dress. . . ."

While at this congenial occupation, "the bristling
halberts of the guard appeared.

"'Back!' screamed Exili. 'Keep off, or I will
slay you and myself, so that not one shall live to tell
the tale! Your lives are in my hands,' continued
the physician, 'and if you move one step forward
they are forfeited.'

"He darted through a doorway at the end of the
room as he spoke, and disappeared. The guard
pressed forward; but, as Exili passed out at the
arch, a mass of timber descended like a portcullis
and opposed their further progress. A loud and
fiendish laugh sounded in the *souterrain*, which
grew fainter and fainter, till they heard it no
more."

The poisoner escaped—for a time. He was cap-
tured afterwards, tried, and, of course, condemned to
death—a merciful death compared with that which
befell him on his way to execution at the hands of
the infuriated people, by whom his guards were
overpowered, and after being almost torn to pieces,
he was thrown into the Seine.

The toils were now closing round the miserable
Marchioness de Brinvilliers. The wretched woman

had reached the inconceivable condition of degrada-
tion said to be common to successful murderers
when impunity has followed their first crimes—that
of killing for killing's sake.   She put on the clothes
of a *religeuse*, attended the hospitals, and poisoned
the patients.   Their dying cries were music to her,
their agonies afforded her the keenest pleasure.   To
the student of French criminal history this is no
news.   I note it here so that the historian of the
woman's crimes should not be thought to have
invented incidents that existed only in his imagination.   Mr. Smith had the best authority for all
the murders with which he charges Madame de
Brinvilliers.

The death of Sainte-Croix was followed by the
usual police regulation where foul play is suspected.
Seals were affixed to his effects, amongst which
poisons were discovered that were proved to be the
property of the Marchioness of Brinvilliers.   The
murderess, terror-stricken, fled from Paris ; and,
though hotly pursued, she escaped into Belgium,
and sought refuge in a religious house, where she
took " sanctuary."   The pursuers were so near that,
as she jumped from her carriage at the convent-
door, she left her cloak in the hands of the exempt.
She turned upon him, says the author, " with a

smile of triumph that threw an expression of
demoniac beauty over her features, and cried :

" 'You dare not touch me, or you are lost body
and soul !' "

I must again refer my reader to Mr. Albert
Smith's book if he wishes to learn how the exempt,
disguised as an abbé, beguiled the Marchioness from
her sanctuary, and content myself with showing—or
rather in letting Leech show—how she looked when
the police-officer dropped his disguise and she found
herself seized by his men.

The details given by Mr. Albert Smith of the last
hours of Madame de Brinvilliers are, though painful
reading, very remarkable. The Docteur Pirot, who
passed nearly the whole of his time at the Con-
ciergerie, has left records of which the author
has availed himself, as well as from the letters of
Madame de Sévigné. Those who wish to "sup
full of horrors" can satisfy themselves by reading
the account of the torture by water which was
inflicted upon the miserable woman to induce her to
betray her accomplices. But there were none to
betray. Her only accomplice was dead. Her
sufferings on the rack very nearly cheated the
headsman, for, as they culminated " in a piercing
cry of agony, after which all was still, the graffier,

fearing that the punishment had been carried too far,
gave orders that she should be unbound." On her
way to execution, she was attended by the constant
Pirot. The tumbrel stopped before the door of
Nôtre Dame, and a paper was put into her hands,
from which she read, in a firm voice, a confession of
her crimes. The tumbrel again advanced with difficulty through the dense crowds, portions of which,
"slipping between the horses of the troops who
surrounded it, launched some brutal remark at Marie
with terrible distinctness and meaning ; but she never
gave the least sign of having heard them, only keeping her eyes intently fixed upon the crucifix which
Pirot held up before her."

In this drawing Leech's power over individual
character may be noted in the diversity of type
amongst the hooting crowd round the tumbrel. The
shrinking form of the prisoner is very beautiful.

When the Place de Grève was reached the
execrations of the mob had ceased, and "a deep
and awful silence" prevailed, "so perfect that the
voices of the executioner and Pirot could be plainly
heard," says the chroniclers. I pass over harrowing
details. The beautiful head of the poisoner was
struck off by a single sword-stroke, and the executioner, turning to Pirot, said :

"'It was well done, monsieur, and I hope madame has left me a trifle, for I deserve it.'"

He then "calmly took a bottle from his pocket and refreshed himself with its contents."

If the short extracts from the history of this great criminal have enabled my readers more clearly to understand and enjoy Leech's illustrations, my object in selecting them has been realized.

CHAPTER X.

"A MAN MADE OF MONEY."—DOUGLAS JERROLD.

KNOWING that this extraordinary book was illustrated by John Leech, and hearing that it contained some of his best work, it became my duty to make a sufficient acquaintance with the book to enable me to criticise and explain the drawings to my readers. I tried "skimming," but the power of the book, and the brilliancy of the wit in it, so attracted me that I read the whole of it.

It is not my province, and it is certainly not in my power, to pose as a critic of literary work ; and the hero—the man made of money, with a heart made of bank-notes instead of flesh and blood, containing within himself a bank that could be drawn upon to any amount—is so wonderful a being as to place him out of the category of human creatures, and altogether beyond criticism. This gentleman's name was Jericho. He had waited till he was forty, and

then he married a widow with three children ; two
of them were girls, the third a young gentleman of
whom those who knew him best said, " He was born
for billiards." There was no love lost between Mr.
Jericho and his step-children ; in fact, they cordially
hated him, and he returned the compliment. Their
name was Pennibacker, inherited from their father,
Captain Pennibacker, whose loving wife " was made a
widow at two-and-twenty by an East Indian bullet."
Mr. Jericho was one of that large class which, though
really needy, manœuvres successfully to be considered wealthy. His step-children considered him
as a rich plum-cake, to be sliced openly or by stealth
among them." The widow Pennibacker was first
attracted to him by " a whispered announcement
that he was a City gentleman. Hence Jericho
appeared to the imagination of the widow with an
indescribable glory of money about him."

Mrs. Jericho desired to make a few purchases, and
she approached her husband with a cry familiar to
most of us :

" ' Mr. Jericho, when can you let me have some
money ?' "

The lady's confidence in her husband's wealth
ought to have been shaken by what followed her
application. Mr. Jericho turned a deaf ear to the

appeal, which was repeated in every variety of tone and accent.

At length, "waving her right hand before her husband's face with a significant and snaky motion," she reiterated her demand with a terrible calmness :

"'When can I have some money?'

"'Woman!' cried Jericho vehemently, as though at once and for ever he emptied his heart of the sex; and, rushing from the room, he felt himself in the flattering vivacity of the moment a single man. ' I'm sure, after all, I do my best to love the woman,' thought Jericho, 'and yet she will ask me for money.'"

Disgusted with these unreasonable demands for money, Mr. Jericho determines to revenge himself by taking a day's pleasure with three special friends, to be ended by "a quiet banquet at which the human heart would expand in good fellowship, and where the wine was above doubt."

The dinner was a great success. It was very late —or rather somewhat early, as the sparrows were twittering from the eaves—when Mr. Jericho sought the marital couch, in which, too, his "wife Sabilla" was evidently "in a sound, deep, sweet sleep."

" Untucking the bed-clothes, and making himself the thinnest slice of a man, Jericho slides between the sheets; and there he lies feloniously still, and he thinks to himself—Being asleep, she cannot tell how late I came to bed. At all events, it is open to dispute, and that is something.

" 'Mr. Jericho, when can you let me have some money?'

" With open eyes, and clearly ringing every word upon the morning air, did Mrs. Jericho repeat this primal question.

"And what said Jericho? With a sudden qualm at the heart, and with a stammering tongue, he answered:

" 'Why, my dear, I thought you were sound asleep.' "

Here follows a dialogue in the vein of the "Caudle Lectures," in which Jerrold gives his wit and humour full play. To the perusal of the "give-and-take" passage of arms I cordially commend my readers. The dialogue closes with these words:

" 'I'm sure it's painful enough to my feelings, and I feel degraded by the question, nevertheless I must and will ask you—*When will you let me have some money?*' "

This was the last straw, and Jericho groaned out:

" 'I WISH TO HEAVEN I WAS MADE OF MONEY!' "

To which Mrs. Jericho retorted, "in a low, deep, earnest voice :

" ' I wish to Heaven you were !' "

Silence came at last, and in the midst of it Jericho "subsided into muddled sleep ; snoring heavily, contemptuously, at the loneliness of his spouse."

And now *two fleas*—an elder and younger flea— come upon the scene, and proceed to dine, or sup, upon Mr. Jericho's brow.

A long conversation ensues between these interesting creatures, in which the elder flea describes to his son how a man's heart was changed into inexhaustible bank-notes.

" ' Miserable race !' said the father flea, with his beautiful bright eye shining pitifully upon Jericho ; 'miserable, craving race, you hear, my son ! Man in his greed never knows when he has wherewithal. He gorges to gluttony ; he drinks to drunkenness ; and you heard this wretched fool who prayed to Heaven to turn him—heart, brain, and all—into a lump of money.' "

How the operation was effected may be learnt from Mr. Jerrold's book. One result of it was a most troubled and miserable night to the dreamer Jericho, whose complaints to his wife when he awoke met with no sympathy.

" ' If I were to live a thousand years, I shouldn't forget last night !' groaned Jericho.

" ' Very likely not,' said Mrs. Jericho ; ' I've no doubt you deserve to remember it. I shouldn't wonder——' "

Mrs. Jericho's want of money is intensified by the wants of her son Basil, whose luck at billiards may have failed him just when his creditors were most pressing.

" ' Well, what does the old fellow say, the scaly old griffin ? What's he got to answer for himself ?' " This was " the sudden question put to Mrs. Jericho on her return to the drawing-room, after the interview with her husband. ' Come, what is it ? Will he give me some money ? In a word,' asked young hopeful, ' will he go into the melting-pot, like a man and a father ?'

" ' My dear Basil, you mustn't ask me,' replied Mrs. Jericho.

" ' Oh, mustn't I, though !' cried Basil. ' Ha, you don't know the lot of people that's asking me ; bless you, they ask a hundred times to my once !' "

The Jerichos have some rich friends, the Carraways, who live in a mansion called Jogtrot Hall, " the one central grandeur, the boast and the comfort of the village of Marigolds." To a fête at the Hall

comes an invitation to the Jerichos.   It had always
been Mrs. Jericho's ambition that her girls should—
" in her own nervous words "—make a blow in
marriage, and she felt that perhaps the time had
come.   But the girls' dresses—the " war-paint," as
Mr. Basil put it—there was the difficulty, only to be
surmounted by Mr. Jericho's yielding to the repeated
cry, " When will you let me have some money ?"

With but faint hopes of success, Mrs. Jericho
seeks her husband in his study.   In a long colloquy,
she urges the importance of her daughters' appearance at this " grand party," and the necessity for an
advance to enable them to do so properly.   Mr.
Jericho turns a deaf ear to her appeal, till suddenly
a wonderful change comes over him.

" Quite a new look of satisfaction gleamed from
his eyes, and his mouth had such a strange smile of
compliance !   What could ail him ?"

The charm was working, the marvellous change
was in operation.   Mrs. Jericho fears for her husband's sanity.   " ' He doesn't look mad,' thought
Mrs. Jericho, a little anxious.

" ' I feel as if I had got new blood, new flesh, new
bones, new brain !   Wonderful !'   Jericho trod up
and down the room and snapt his fingers.   ' Something's going to happen,' said he."

And something did indeed happen. The transformation was complete ; the hard heart had given
place to illimitable money.

" 'You will let me have the money ?' repeated
Mrs. Jericho.

" Jericho answered not a word, but withdrew his
hand from his breast. Between his finger and his
thumb he held in silver purity a virgin Bank of
England note for a hundred pounds. Mrs. Jericho
ran delightedly off with the money.

" And Jericho sat with his heart beating faster.
Again he placed his hand to his breast, again drew
forth another bank-note. He jumped to his feet,
tore away his dress, and, running to a mirror, saw
therein reflected, not human flesh, but over the
region of the heart a loose skin of bank-paper,
veined with marks of ink. He touched it, and still
in his hand lay another note. His thoughtless wish
had been wrought into reality. Solomon Jericho
was in very truth a Man made of Money."

The fête at Jogtrot Hall was a great success.
The guests were many, and some of them distinguished. The Honourable Mr. Candytuft, Colonel
Bones, Commissioner Thrush, and Dr. Mizzlemist, of
Doctors' Commons, must be noted, as they have to
be dealt with pictorially by Leech hereafter. After

a variety of entertainments, some twenty or thirty
hungry guests graced a table under a long, wide
tent, on which " there were the most delicious proofs
of the earth's goodness, with every kitchen mystery."
The host, Mr. Carraway, took the head of the
table ; Mr. Jericho, "dignified and taciturn, graced
the board." The orator on the occasion was Dr.
Mizzlemist, who had been seized with a passion to
drink everybody's health. For the third time he
rose to give " the health of Solomon Jericho,
Esquire, an honour to his country."

" In the course of his speech the Doctor delivered
himself with so much energy that at the same time
he stuck the fork, which had served him in empha-
sizing the Jericho virtues, between the bones of Mr.
Jericho's right hand, pinning it where it lay.

" ' It is nothing,' said the philosophic Jericho."

The change in Mr. Jericho's appearance, from the
full-faced, healthy-looking individual of Leech's first
drawing, to the spare, hollow-cheeked man at the
banquet, is to be accounted for by the fact that,
after each application to the strange bank established
in Mr. Jericho's breast, his whole form shrinks;
he becomes thinner and thinner, to the alarm of his
tailor, who " says, as he measures the changed
man :

" ' Six inches less round the body, as I'm a sinner! Six inches less, Mr. Jericho, and I last took your measure six weeks ago.' "

At the Carraway fête the Misses Jericho made, and improved, the acquaintance of the Hon. Mr. Candytuft, and of an incredible idiot, Sir Arthur Homadod. The idiot was as beautiful as he was foolish; he was therefore handsome beyond the dreams of beauty. Whatever had taken the place of the mind in the baronet was impressed by Miss Agatha Pennibacker, and that virgin's heart being free, she lost it to Sir Arthur. The Hon. Mr. Candytuft, having an eye to the enormous fortune supposed to be possessed by Mr. Jericho, and being desirous to secure the portion of it that would of course fall to his step-daughter, made love to Miss Monica with considerable success.

In the meantime the ladies wish to go to Court; in this they are encouraged by Candytuft; and, to enable them to make a proper figure there, costly jewels are required. To Candytuft and Jericho enter Mrs. J., " with a magnificent suite of jewels.

" ' Aren't they beautiful, my dear Solomon ?' said she. . . .

" ' You know, my dear,' said Mrs. Jericho, in her sweetest, most convincing voice, ' it would be

impossible to go to Court without diamonds.   One
isn't dressed without diamonds.'

"'Court!' Jericho opened his eyes, and a wan
smile broke on his thin, blank cheek. 'Are you
going to Court?'

"'Why, of course—are we not, dear Mr. Candytuft? What would be thought of us if we did not
pay our homage to——'

"The sentence was broken by the sudden appearance of Monica and Agatha, each bearing a jewel-
case, and looking radiant with the possession.

"'Thank you, dear papa,' said Monica, curtseying
and smiling her best to Jericho.

"'They're beautiful. Thank you—dear, dearest
papa,' cried the more impulsive Agatha.

"'Look!' said Monica, and she exhibited her
treasure.

"'Look!' cried Agatha, and she half dropped upon
one knee, on the other side, to show her jewels.

"'Beautiful!' cried Candytuft. 'Pray, ladies, don't
stir.'

"The girls, with pretty wonder on their faces,
kept their positions on either side of Jericho.

"'My dear madam'—and Candytuft appealed to
Mrs. Jericho—'is not this a delightful group—an
exquisite family picture?   It ought to be painted.'"

A Family Picture

Mr. Candytuft is right. The graceful figures of the girls, the attenuated figure of papa, in whose hopeless expression one sees the dread of further attenuation, together with his own perfect presentment, would make—indeed, does make—an admirable picture. The jewels cost one thousand pounds : ten calls have to be made upon the supernatural bank. They are made, and the jeweller is paid. And the result ! For some minutes after the departure of the tradesman Jericho sat motionless — all but breathless. He would, however, know his fate. He took out the silk lace with which an hour ago he had measured his chest. Again he passed it round his body. He had drawn upon the bank, and he had shrunk an inch.

Truly he was a man made of money—money was the principle of his being, for with every note he paid away a portion of his life.

Poor Mr. Carraway was ruined through no fault of his own. Jogtrot Hall was sold, and Jericho bought it. Thirty thousand pounds' worth of flesh had he sacrificed to buy to himself a country mansion. He had become a member of Parliament, and at the same time become so thin that his tailor declared, "It's like measuring a penknife for a sheath." "Why," said the tailor to his wife, "he

isn't a man at all, but a cotton‑pod.   He can't
have no more stomach than a 'bacco‑pipe."   In fact,
it was the growing belief of a large circle that
Jericho was no flesh, no man, at all.   "He was
made up of coats," ran the rumour, "like an
onion."

The insolence that is sometimes the accompani‑
ment of great riches took full possession of Mr.
Jericho, and he found an occasion to treat Colonel
Bones to a specimen of it.   Almost without provo‑
cation the Colonel was called "a toad-eater! a bone-
picking pauper!" etc.   For this insult the Colonel
declared he would have Mr. Jericho's blood, and in
pursuance of that object he sent the millionaire a
challenge.   Jericho fought very hard to avoid
fighting, but his second, Mr. Candytuft, prevailed,
and the belligerents met in Battersea Fields.   Mr.
Commissioner Thrush waited upon the angry Colonel,
and the celebrated Dr. Dodo was there to attend to
the wounded.   The seconds confer ; the men are
placed.   Candytuft looked at them with an eye of
admiration.   The signal was given.

"Colonel Bones fires, and his ball goes clear
through Jericho's bosom, knocking off a button in
its passage, and striking itself flat against a pile of
bricks."

"'A dead man!' cried the doctor, running to Jericho.

"'My friend,' exclaimed Candytuft, 'have you made your will?'

"'Eh? What's the matter?' said Jericho.

"'Matter!' exclaimed Dr. Dodo, and he pointed his cane to the hole in the front of Jericho's coat, immediately over the region of his heart. 'Matter! It's the first time I ever heard a man with a bullet clean through his breast ask—What's the matter!'"

The Colonel's ball had passed through Jericho's bank-note-paper breast, and Jericho lived and moved and was none the worse for it. Jericho fired in the air.

An ugly atmosphere was collecting about Mr. Jericho, and he was aware of it. "His own family saw in him a man of mysterious attributes. Monica turned pale at the smallest courtesy of her parent, and Agatha, suddenly meeting him on the staircase, squealed and ran away as from a fiend.

"Mr. Jericho went on a rejoicing conqueror. His huge town mansion, burning with gold—massive, rich, and gorgeous; for the Man of Money was far the most substantial, the most potent development of his creed, whereby to awe and oppress his worshippers——"

Mrs. Jericho had made up her mind that it was time her daughters were " settled in life, and she said as much to her husband."

" ' Your girls, my dear, have my free permission to settle when and where they like,' said the hus- band.

" But in sounding Mr. Jericho as to his intentions in the matter of settlements, she could make no way whatever. At last she put the point-blank question :

" ' What do you propose to give the dear child ?' (alluding to Monica, for whose hand Candytuft was about to ask).

" ' Give ! I'll give a magnificent party on the occasion.'

" ' But the dowry ; what dowry do you give ?'

" ' Dowry ! I thought, my dear, you observed marriage was no bargain ? Why, you're making it quite a ready-money transaction !' "

At this point the conversation was interrupted by Mr. Candytuft, who, before advocating his own case, warmly espoused that of his foolish friend, Sir Arthur Homadod, the accepted of Agatha.

" ' He's as bashful as—as—upon my life I am at a loss for a simile. And as he and I are old friends, and as he knew that I should see you—in fact, he's in the house at this moment, and came along with me

—he desired me to inform you that Miss Agatha had consented to fix the—the—what d'ye call it—the happy day.'

" ' Wish them joy,' said Jericho.

" ' As to the young lady's dowry?' hesitated Candytuft.

" ' I can't give a farthing ; can't afford it, my dear Candytuft.' "

The ambassador then speaks for himself :

" ' You may have remarked my affection for Miss Monica ?   You must have remarked it ?'

" ' I beg a thousand pardons,' said the wag Jericho, ' but it has quite escaped me.'

" Candytuft wanly smiled.

" ' In a word, my dear sir, we have come to the sweet conclusion that we were made for one another.'

" ' Dear me !   Well, how lucky you should have met !' "

Mr. Candytuft beats about the bush for awhile, but at last comes abruptly to the point, saying :

" ' I *must* ask—you force me to be plain—what will you give with the young lady ?'

" ' Not a farthing !' cried Jericho.   ' Not one farthing !' said the man of money with determined emphasis.

" ' What is the matter?' said Mrs. Jericho, who entered the room at this juncture.

" ' Pooh! you know well enough,' cried Jericho. ' Mr. Candytuft wants to marry rich; but that's not all—he wants to be handsomely paid for the trouble.' "

After awhile Jericho affects to agree to dower his step-daughter, and he says :

" ' Let us settle the sum, eh! Well, then, what sum would satisfy you?' "

It was a delicate question to put thus nakedly.

" ' Come, name a figure. Say five thousand pounds.' "

Candytuft looked blankly at Jericho, moving not a muscle.

" ' What do you say to seven?'

" Candytuft gently lifted his eyebrows, deprecating the amount.

" ' Come, then, we'll advance to ten?'

" The lover's face began to thaw, and he showed some signs of kindly animation.

" ' At a word, then,' cried Jericho with affected heartiness, ' will you take fifteen thousand?'

" ' From you—yes,' cried Candytuft ; and he seized Jericho's hand.

" The man of money looked at Candytuft with a

contemptuous sneer, and with a wrench twisted his
hand away.   He then dropped into a chair, and a
strange, diabolical scowl possessed his countenance.
The man of money looked like a devil.

" ' And where—where do you think this money is
to come from ?   Where ?' asked Jericho, and he rose
from his chair, and it seemed as though the demon
possessing him would compel the wretch to talk—
would compel him to make terrible revelations.   Each
word he uttered was born of agony.   But there he
stood, forced to give utterances that tortured him.
' I will tell you,' roared Jericho, ' what this money is.
Look about you !   What do you see ?—fine pictures,
fine everything.   Why, you see me—tortured, torn,
worked up, changed.   The walls are hung with my
flesh—my flesh you walk upon.   I am worn piece-
meal by a hundred thieves, but I'll be shared among
them no longer.' "

By this time the girls and Sir Arthur Homadod,
alarmed by the cries of Jericho, had entered the
room.

" ' And you had a fine feast, had you not ?' cried
the possessed man of money, writhing with misery
and howling his confession.   ' And what did you
eat ?—my flesh.   What did you drink ?—my blood !' "

It would be impossible to imagine a more satisfactory realization of this powerful scene than Leech's rendering of it. The shrinking figure of Candytuft as he retreats before the fury of the moneyed man ; the awful passion of the shrivelled Jericho ; above all, the vacuous expression of Sir Arthur, all are done to perfection and without exaggeration. Beyond the endeavour to make the meaning of the illustrations in the "Man made of Money" clear to my readers, I have little or nothing to do with the story. I may note, however, that young Basil Pennibacker falls in love with Bessy, the pretty daughter of the ruined merchant Carraway, and that bold bankrupt, who is about to seek a new fortune at the Antipodes, calls upon Jericho to ask his consent to his stepson's marriage. How the announcement of the engagement was received may be imagined, or if my reader be not satisfied with his idea of what may have taken place, he can read in Mr. Jerrold's book how Mr. Carraway was met by his old friend. He will also find an illustration of an interview between "The Pauper and the Man of Money," but as I do not think it quite worthy of Leech, I do not reproduce it. I may as well add that Basil—who turns out to be a very good fellow—does marry Bessy, and the happy pair, with the parent pair of Carraways, depart for Australia in the good ship *Halcyon*.

Mr. Jericho's explosion, and his unpleasant conduct
generally—especially regarding Monica's dowry—
had altered Mr. Candytuft's matrimonial intentions
for the present : there were delays. " He had suddenly discovered some dormant right to some long-
forgotten property, and he meant to secure that, and
lay it as an offering at the feet of his bride." How
the foolish Sir Arthur agreed to marry Agatha without a dowry, to the intense delight of Jericho—how
splendid preparations for the wedding were made—
how the wedding-party, Jericho included, waited
at the church for the bridegroom, who never came
(he had overslept himself in consequence of an over-
dose of medicine taken to steady his nerves)—for
these details my reader is again referred to Mr.
Jerrold, who describes the whole most enjoyably.
Leech draws the baronet awakened by his servant,
but too late : the canonical hour has passed. A report was spread that Sir Arthur had taken poison to
avoid the Jericho connection.

Just at this time Mr. Jericho was offered a most
satisfactory mortgage—so any way there was land
for his money—no less than five-and-forty thousand
pounds, by his friend the Duke of St. George.

Jericho lent the money, in the hope of climbing
into the House of Lords with the assistance of the

Duke; but this last drain upon his resources, with
its penalty of attenuation, had left very little of him
to go anywhere.

"He had shrunk," says the author. "How
horribly he had dwindled, how wretchedly small he
had become! Ay, how small! He would measure
himself, he would know the exact waste. Whereupon Jericho took the silken cord and passed it
round his breast. Why, it would twice encircle him
—twice! and a piece to spare. With horror and
loathing he flung the cord into the fire. He would
never again take damning evidence against himself."

It became evident to Jericho that, if he desired to
retain enough of his person to enable his friends and
relations to recognise him, the drain upon the chest
notes must cease.

"He would, therefore, not draw another note—
no, not another. He would live upon what he had.
He would turn the foolish superfluities about him
into hard, tangible money."

Bent upon turning everything belonging not only
to himself, but to his wife and daughters, into cash,
he sent for Mrs. Jericho.

"The trembling wife had scarcely power to meet
the eyes of her helpmate. In two days twenty years

seemed to have gathered upon him. His face looked brown, thin, and withered as last year's leaf. His whole body bent and swayed like a piece of paper moved by the air. As he held his hand aloof, the light shone through it. It was plain there was some horrid compact between her lord and the infernal powers, or — it was all as one — the tyranny of conscience had worn him to his present condition.

" ' Mrs. Jericho, madam, you will instantly bring me all your diamonds—jewellery—all. Give like orders to your daughters, the mincing harpies that eat me.' "

The terrified woman remonstrated, asked for an explanation, offered to send for the doctor.

" ' Away with you ! do as I command. Bring me all your treasures—all. And your minxes ! See that they obey me too, and instantly.'

" ' Yes, my love, to be sure,' said Mrs. Jericho, for she was all but conviced that Solomon's reason was gone or going. It was best to humour him. ' And why, my love, do you wish for these things ? Of course you shall have them, but why ?'

" ' To turn them into money, madam,' cried Jericho, rubbing his hands. ' We have had enough of the tomfoolery of wealth—I now begin to hunger for the substance. I'll do without fashion. I'll have power, madam—power!' "

The conversation continued, and Mrs. Jericho became more and more convinced that her husband was mad.

"'Oh that Dr. Stubbs would make a morning call!' silently prayed the wife."

The man of money, having determined to dismantle his house and send his wife and daughters adrift, retired with one servant, all the rest being discharged, into "one of his garrets, a den of a place," where the scullion had slept. The servant was the pauper grandfather of one of his footmen, an old man of "congenial weakness with Jericho. Indeed, there looked between them a strange similitude, twin brethren damned to the like sordidness, the like rapacity."

Jericho had nicknamed the old man Plutus. Jericho and Plutus were in face and expression as like as two snakes.

Mrs. Jericho, assured of her husband's madness, took counsel with her friends. Drs. Stubbs and Mizzlemist, Colonel Bones, Commissioner Thrush, and Candytuft met in conclave and listened to Mrs. Jericho's account of her husband's ravings ; but she failed to convince the doctors that what a jury would

consider insanity, was apparent in anything that the
man of money had said or done.   As Dr.
Mizzlemist delivered this opinion, a crash was heard
in an adjoining room—another, and another, and
then a loud triumphant laugh from the throat of
Jericho.

Wife and daughters, with jury of friends, started
to their feet.   Candytuft, ere he was aware—for had
he reflected "a moment, he would as soon have
unbarred a lion's cage — opened the doors.   And
there stood Jericho, laden with spoil."

Though Mr. Jericho was voted sane by the
doctors, his conduct displayed a brutality for which
madness would be the only excuse.   The Jews were
coming, everything was to be sold.

" 'Why stay you here?' cried the man of money
to his wife.   'Why will you not be warned?   In a
few hours there will not be a bed for your fine costly
bones to lie upon.   Now will you depart?' "

The Jews wandered about the rooms, appraising
everything.   Jericho was anxious to avoid a "public
hubbub," as he called a sale.

" 'I want,' said he to the brokers, 'at a thought,
to melt all you see, and have seen, into ready
money.   Take counsel together, I say, and make
me an offer, a lumping offer, for the whole—eh?' "

'And there stood Jericho.'

The man of money ascended to his garret and awaited the Jews' offer, which was promised for the evening. He was alone, " evening closed in, and the moon rose and looked reproachfully at the miser."

The garret door opened, and Plutus appeared.

" ' Well, has it come ?' cried the master.

" ' Here it is,' answered the servant, as he laid a letter upon the table.

" ' Well, now for their conscience !' exclaimed the man of money."

Light was required ; there was a candle upon the table, and paper prepared to light it.

" Most precious paper — the heart's flesh and blood of the man of money! For the devilish serving-man had folded a note (how obtained can it matter ?)—a note peeled from the breast of his master, a piece of money, a part of the damned Jericho sympathizing with him.

" The man of money took the paper—the devil, with his ear upturned, crept closer to the door—and thrust it amidst the dying coals. A moment, and the garret is rent as with a lightning flash.

" Yelling, and all on fire, the man of money falls prostrate with hell in his face. Then his lips move, but not a sound is heard. And the fire communicated by the sympathy of the living note—the flesh of his flesh—like a snake of flame glides up his limbs, devouring them.   And so he is consumed : a minute, and the man of money is a thin black paper ash.   Now the night wind stirs it, and now a sudden breeze carries the cinereous corpse away, fluttering it to dust impalpable."

CHAPTER XI.

ALBERT SMITH AND LEECH.

In July, 1851, a new work appeared, under the name and title of the *Month :* "a View of Passing Subjects and Manners, Home and Foreign, Social and General, by Albert Smith and John Leech." The publication was a serial one — monthly, in fact ; and as it contained many amusing skits by Albert Smith, and much of Leech's best work, notice of it is incumbent upon a writer of Leech's life.

Eighteen fifty-one, as everybody knows, was the year of the Great Crystal Palace Exhibition in Hyde Park. . I well remember visiting the huge glass building in February, 1851, in company with Dickens and Sir Joseph Paxton. Dickens was wrapped in furs, and we shivered through the place, which was only partially roofed ; and seemed altogether so far from completion as to cause great doubts in our minds of the possibility of its being ready for its contents by the first of May.

I put the question to Paxton, and his reply was :

" I *think* it will ; but, mind, I don't *say* it will."

Paxton's thought was justified ; for the Exhibition was opened by the Queen in great state at the date fixed, though many of its intended exhibits were still to come.

I confess I shared the foolish dread that the opening would be so crowded as to be very uncomfortable, if not dangerous, to sight-seers ; and I therefore declined to accompany my brother, who was braver than I ; and sorry enough I was when I found that the panic had been so universal as to enable the few courageous visitors to have the show, as my brother expressed it, "all to themselves."

The first number of the *Month* appeared in July, 1851, and the last was issued towards the close of that year. It seems to have been the intention of the authors to have taken typical young ladies, and, under the heading of " Belles of the Month," have used them as prefixes to each monthly part. Unfortunately, I think this idea was only partially carried out. True, we have Belles of

the Park, and Belles of the Ball, and one or two
Belles of the Month, so charmingly done by Leech
as to make it a matter of surprise that such great
attractions were not more frequently admitted to the
paper.

The literary portion which begins the *Month* is
very Albert Smithian indeed. In proof, I quote
some of his description of "The Hyde Park
Belle":

"The charming young lady introduced to me,"
says Mr. Smith, "was of middling stature, with
oval face, chestnut hair, dark eyes, and very white
and regular teeth. She had on a white transparent
bonnet, and light muslin dress all *en suite*. In
answer to my questions, she replied as follows:

"'I shall be nineteen in August, and have been
out two years and a half. Have I ever been
engaged? Only once, and that was broken off
because I went on a drag to Richmond with the
officers of the —th. Lady Banner was inside—it
was all perfectly proper. She is a very nice woman
—always ready to chaperone anybody anywhere if
her share is paid. Only sometimes she bores one
dreadfully. Edmund went to India. I don't know
where he is now; I have not heard. I dare say he
is somewhere. He bored me dreadfully at last.

I work very hard—oh, very hard indeed!—that is, in the season. My maid always sits up to make tea for me when I come home. Her hours are very regular, considering. She goes to bed every morning about four; but, then, she doesn't have to dance half the night. Yes; I like the Crystal Palace. Oh! I get so tired there—walking, and walking, and walking, you can't think how far! I know the Crystal Palace fountain and Dent's clock, and the stuffed animals and the envelope-machine. I don't think I have seen anything else; I have never been out of the nave and the transept— nobody goes anywhere else. I did not know that there was anything to see upstairs, except large carpets. I am sure they would bore me dreadfully. We are engaged every night. . . . We had scarcely time to dress for the Grapnels' dinner-party; and then we went to Mrs. Crutchley's, to meet the Lapland Ambassador. We could not get into the room, and stood for two hours on the landing. Old Mr. Tawley was there, and would keep talking to me; he always bores me dreadfully. He is going to take mamma and me to see some pictures somewhere. I hate seeing pictures; they bore me dreadfully. After Lady Crutchley's, we went to Mrs. Croley's amateur concert, which was nearly

over. She had only classical music. I don't know
what classical music is ; I only know it bores me
dreadfully. Ashton Howard says the same people
who like classical music buy old china and wear
false hair. I wish people would give up classical
music. It never amuses anybody—that is, anybody worth amusing. I don't know whether " The
Huguenots " is classical music or not ; I only know
that when they give it at the Royal Italian Opera
nobody seems bored *then*. I don't know that I am
exactly.' "

Whether in these boxes full of beauties one
amongst them is intended by Leech to personate
Mr. Smith's " dreadfully bored " young lady, I
cannot say. Certainly there is not one who seems
in the condition described as not being " exactly
bored."

The Belle of Hyde Park continues :

" ' I go into the Park every day with mamma,
but it bores me dreadfully. I see nothing but the
same people, and I know all the trees and rails by
heart. I ride sometimes ; I like it better than the
carriage. But papa don't ride very often ; and if
he don't I can't, except with the Pevenseys and
their brothers. John Pevensey is very stupid, and
talks to me about farming. I get very tired ; but

I am obliged to go, because the Pevenseys know so many receivable people. But they bore me dreadfully; in fact, I don't know who or what does not. I long for the season to be over; and when I go into the country, I long for it to begin again. I wish I could do as I pleased, like Marshall—that's my maid—when she has a holiday. She is going to marry the man at the hairdresser's; and last Sunday they went down all by themselves to Gravesend. I see mamma's face if Ashton Howard was to propose to take me to Gravesend next Sunday, and without Lady Banner! I wish sometimes I was Marshall. Now and then I would give a good deal for a good cry. I can't tell you why— I don't know; only that everything is a trouble, and bores me dreadfully.'"

In reply to further inquiries from Mr. Smith, the young lady tells him what she pays for her satin shoes, which are worn out after two parties. Does she have her gloves cleaned?

"'Certainly; but not for evening parties—the men's coats blacken them in an instant. They do very well for the opera and evening concerts— nothing else. The Pevenseys wear cleaned gloves. Everybody knows it; and Ashton Howard always asks out loud if a camphine-lamp has gone out when they come into the room. You can get a nice bouquet for five or six shillings. Old Mr. Rigby, in the Regent's Park, told me I might cut any flowers from his conservatory. But I don't care for that—I would sooner buy them ; he bores me dreadfully.' "

It cannot be denied that ugliness has reached its climax in men's dress of the present day. It would be extremely difficult to find a garment more hideous than a dress-coat ; and it is impossible for any head-covering to exceed the stove-pipe hat in ugliness, to say nothing of inconvenience and detestable uncomfortableness.

These sentiments were fully shared by one of the *Month's* correspondents, a gentleman named Simmons, who " emerged from his residence at Islington " on the day of the opening of the Great Exhibition with the intention of showing to the multitudes who were expected to attend that cere- mony the kind of hat that should depose, at once and for ever, the detestable chimney-pot.

" It was, in fact," says the bold reformer, " merely a wide-brimmed, flat-crowned wideawake, to which I thought a feather—in these days of foreign im- migration—would not be an out-of-the-way addition. I had contemplated my own features beneath it in as much variety of light and shadow as I could obtain from my shaving-glass for half an hour preceding. my departure, and had arrived at such a satisfactory conclusion as to its effect, that I regarded myself as a sort of modern William Tell, about to release my country, by a bold example, from an oppressive and degrading subjection to a detested hat."

A love of change is said to be inherent in human nature ; but attacks upon custom—indeed, innovations of all kinds—are usually futile unless very special conditions attend the attempts. If the famous hat invented by a Royal Prince was received with overwhelming ridicule, as my older readers will remember that it was ; a less melancholy fate could scarcely be expected for the wideawake and feather of the little gentleman from Islington.

"My appearance in the street certainly created a sensation," says Mr. Simmons ; "but it was one exceedingly mortifying to my feelings. Omnibus drivers winked at each other, and pointed at me with their whips. Occasionally a stray boy would indulge in personal observations, or a grown-up ragamuffin would sputter out an oath, and burst into a horse laugh, which to my mind appeared totally unwarranted by the circumstances of the case.

The managers of the *Month* very wisely placed
this etching in the front of their first number. In
all respects Leech is here seen at his best. The
figure of the poor little victim of reform, the street-
boys and their surroundings, are all unsurpassable;
while to an artist the composition of the figures and
the arrangement of light and shadow are excellent.

After escaping from the attentions of Leech's
inimitable Arabs, Mr. Simmons reaches Hyde Park
to find fresh troubles. The feathered wideawake
creates a sensation, but not of the kind that its
wearer expected; he was asked where "he bought
it," and "if he would sell it"; "if he made it himself";
and if he had "another at home like it to spare for a
friend," and so on. The "air of unconsciousness"
that the reformer assumed irritated his assailants,
whose "offensive remarks and insolent mirth" were
soon exchanged for attentions more uncomfortable.

Says Mr. Simmons: "A bright flash of practical
jocularity suddenly illumined the mind of an original
genius, who at once carried it into effect by casting
at my decided article of costume a large tuft of grass,
which struck me on the back of my neck, broke into
dry dirt, and raised a perfect roar of delight at my
expense." Instead of patiently enduring this assault,
as a prudent man would have done when surrounded

Mr. Simmon's attempt at Reform

by enemies, the valiant Simmons turned upon his
assailant, "and struck the wit a severe blow in the
face." That was a death-blow to the picturesque
hat, which "afforded some slight sport as a foot-
ball for a few moments, and then vanished and was
seen no more."

It will be seen by the quotations that the literary
portion of the *Month* is of the slight character—
though sometimes clever and amusing—to which so
much of Leech's work has been allied. A sketch,
entitled "Home from the Party," gives occasion for
the accompanying drawing by Leech of a young
gentleman who has "danced all night till the broad
daylight," "and gone home" by himself "in the
morning." On his journey a brougham overtakes
him, containing "the handsome dark girl with the
clematis and fuchsia wreath, looking pale and pretty,
with a pocket-handkerchief over her head corner-
wise, held together at the chin. We think about
that brougham-girl till she is out of sight, and
wonder if we appeared to the best advantage as
she passed. We don't much think we did. One
of the springs of our hat was out of order, and we
were carrying our gloves in our hand, crumpled up
to the size of a walnut, as though we were going to
conjure with them ; and we were blinking as we met

the sun at the corner, and holding a seedy bouquet in our hand, which evidently she had not given us."

The remarks, conversations, comments, and so forth, that generally accompany Leech's drawings were invariably his own composition, and in their humorous aptness are almost as admirable as the drawings they explain. In illustration I note a design under the heading of "Moral Courage."

"SCENE—*A Station of the Shoeblack Brigade.*

"FIRST BOY: 'Here's another swell, Bill, a-coming to be blacked.'

"SECOND BOY: 'Ooray!'

"THIRD BOY: 'Ain't his boots thin neither?'

"FOURTH BOY: 'Wouldn't they pinch my toes if I had 'em? Oh my!'

"FIFTH BOY: 'They don't pinch his'n.'

"SIXTH BOY: 'Yes, they do.'

"FIRST BOY: 'Go easy, Blacky; mind his corns.' (*Swell winces.*) 'That was a nasty one.'

"(*The comments are extended from the swell's boots to his costume and appearance generally. And all this for a penny*)."

Mr. Thackeray's "Four Georges" are, no doubt, familiar to my readers, some of whom may also remember his delivery of them in the form of lectures to large audiences. In that great writer's early time he wrote many essays, art-criticisms, etc., under the name of "Michael Angelo Titmarsh," and it is under that title that he is represented in the drawing by his friend Leech, as he appeared at Willis's Rooms "in his celebrated character of Mr. Thackeray."

In the *Month*, Mr. Albert Smith makes Leech's drawing a peg upon which he hangs some justly complimentary remarks on the Thackeray lectures which took the town by storm forty years ago.

Whether the "Belle of Hyde Park" or the "Belle of the Ball" is to be considered the belle of the *Month's* July issue is left in doubt; but there is no doubt whatever about the claim of the pretty creature (who, accompanied by an extremely plain and disso-lute-looking cavalier in the costume of Charles II.'s time, enters an imaginary ball-room) to a loveliness that it would be difficult to surpass, as the drawing amply proves.

This cut is accompanied by some verses which appear to me quite unreadable; I therefore spare my readers from the infliction of any of them.

The frontispiece to the *Month* for August is an etching by Leech of singular beauty, called "Charade Acting." I have looked in vain through the letter-press for any explanation of this charade, so I suppose the meaning is purposely left for discovery to the intelligence of the observer. It represents the clever performance of Mr. Smiley and Miss Corgy.

Mr. Smiley evidently represents a valorous knight
—else why that dish-cover shield, that saucepan
helmet, that long surcoat of nightshirt in the place of
mail ? The knight has armed himself further with
sword and lance (sword of any period, lance a roast-
ing-spit). Those warlike preparations must have
been made in defence of that delicious girl leaning
over the back of the ancient chair. Is she supposed
to be a distressed damsel leaning from her prison-
window and listening to Mr. Smiley's vows of
liberating her or dying in the attempt ? If so,
where is the word that will express as much ? Not
in the brain of the stout old gentleman who is fast
asleep amongst the audience, nor in that of the
pretty little girl who sits in front of him apparently
wondering why people should be " so silly." The
lady who tries to hide a yawn with her fan has
evidently "given it up," and the two lovely women
near her are much in the same condition.

Now we come to the belle of the month of
August, who is riding with her papa in Kensington
Gardens. An attempt was made—later, I think,
than the Exhibition year—to extend Rotten Row
into Kensington Gardens, and thus deprive pedes-
trians—notably children and nursemaids—of their
promenades amongst the trees. For some months

the equestrian habitués of Rotten Row careered in
the Gardens, to the terror and danger of children,
and the disturbance of many groups of soldiers and
nursemaids.   This usurpation created very strong
opposition.

I lived in the neighbourhood, and I accompanied a deputation to Sir Cornewall Lewis —
then in power—with a view of impressing upon that
Minister the desirability of rescinding the objectionable privilege which had been granted to the riders.
We had some eloquent talkers, but their oratory
seemed to me to make no impression upon Sir C.
Lewis, who may have listened, but during the
harangues he was always writing letters, and no
sooner was one finished than he began another ; and
we left him without an intimation of our success or
failure.   But what is certain is, that within a week
of our interview the equestrians disappeared—I hope
for ever—from Kensington Gardens.   Leech being
a constant rider, both spoke and drew in favour of
the new ride.   Drawings may be found in the *Punch*
series in which he laughs at the opponents of the
horses in the Gardens, and I remember his indignation when I told him of our deputation and its
successful issue.

Leech was never happier than in the infinite

THE BELLE OF THE MONTH—AUGUST—TAKING A "CONSTITUTIONAL" IN
KENSINGTON GARDENS. TIME, 8 A.M.

variety of his pictures of life at the seaside; his
invention was inexhaustible, as numberless groups
of seaside visitors engaged in the search of
health or pleasure — from the small digger on
the sands to the valetudinarian at the Spa —
sufficiently prove. Never was he more delightful
than in dealing with the charming lady bathers,
one of whom plays the part of the *Month's* "Belle
of September."

I think this picture might have inspired the poet
of the *Month*, but his lyre is silent.

"The Balcony Nuisance!" Without some explanation the drawing that follows this title would be
perfectly incomprehensible. How, in the name of
common-sense, of propriety, or of justice, can the
word "nuisance" be applicable to the occupants of
that balcony ? Well, it is in this wise : A corre-
spondent of the *Month*, who signs himself "Narcissus," lives in a suburban square, from which he
indites a remarkable letter. According to "Narcissus," suburban squares are famous for the production of vast numbers of "single ladies." He
calls his square a "realm of girldom," the proportion
of the belles being very great over the marriageable
young men, and therefore they watch with keen
eyes for any new flirtations. "And now," said he,

"comes my complaint.   I cannot call at any house
where there are daughters but, the instant I knock,

THE BALCONY NUISANCE.

every balcony near me is filled with waves of rustling
muslin, and a dozen pairs of bright eyes are on the

qui vive for every movement or expression. I need not say how annoying this is."

I see no trace of annoyance in the simpering buck who is the cynosure of all eyes in the drawing. Leech evidently saw through the affectation of annoyance, and depicted the Narcissus mind in its real condition of gratified conceit.

The *Month's* October issue contains a good deal of Leech's work. The number contains a " Belle of the Month," but she is so inferior in attractiveness to her sisters that I am ungallant enough to pass her by. I find, however, a pretty musical group entitled " Pestal." In 1851 Mr. Albert Smith says that Pestal, who was a Russian officer, was imprisoned for marrying without the consent of his Sovereign, and " cast for death." Of course, though, according to Mr. Smith, this unfortunate man may have been a " Pestal-ent person," we are not expected to believe the crime for which he was executed was only that of neglecting to ask the Czar's consent to his marriage. " On the eve of his execution, as he lay *ironed*, awaiting the next morning's *mangling*," continues the inveterate punster, "in a happy moment of enthusiasm, he composed the waltz that bears his name."

The pretty music seems to have sentimentalized

the handsome youth, and drawn him closer to the
performer, who is one of those sweet creatures with
whom the artist has made us so familiar. I cannot
refrain from presenting my readers with an example
of the *poetry* that adorns the *Month*, so that they may
be convinced of the propriety of giving them as little
of it as possible. Forty-one verses, of which the
two following are fair examples, accompany the
drawing called Pestal :

> "In London, as usual, last season I spent,
>   To Pocklington Square my notes were addressed all,
> And wherever I rambled or wandered or went,
>   I was pestered with that horrid pest of a ' Pestal.'

> " I thought this mysterious, moreover, and queer,
>   'Tis better at once that the truth be confest all—
> That all through the city one word should appear,
>   And that word the incomprehensible ' Pestal.' "

" The Great Dinner-Bell Nuisance " not only
gives occasion for a capital drawing by Leech, but
the title also heads a capital paper, in which the
absurdity of the function, when there is not the least
necessity for it, is well satirized. A retired lawyer
named Watkins Brown lives in a village which
contains at most 347 people, " in a comfortable sort
of house in the Italian style, which he christened
Somerford Villa." He has no children, and his

establishment consists of five persons, Mrs. W. B.,
Betsy, the cook, etc., including Buttons, the page.
This boy, armed with a bell, is a nuisance to the
neighbourhood ; he performs upon it three times a
day. "Now," says the indignant writer, "why does
Buttons do this? Is it to echo back the sound that
comes at the same hours from Sir Marmaduke
Hamilton's, of Somerford Hall, and to impress
people that Brown and Sir Marmaduke are the only
gentlemen in the neighbourhood? It can't be to
let Brown and his wife know that luncheon or dinner
is ready, for in nine cases out of ten they are in the
room when the cloth is laid. Again I ask, why
does Buttons do this? If he is of opinion that his
master is unaware it is time to dress for dinner, why
doesn't he tell him so at once when he is in the
room, instead of using such an absurd system of
information? However, by six o'clock Brown and
his wife are in the drawing-room, and Buttons seeing
them there, and perceiving that they are just about
to go to the dining-room, rushes out to the little
court-yard, and then to the door of the miniature
conservatory, and again commits the offence he had
committed half an hour before. In the baby court-
yard there are two dogs chained, and two other
sporting dogs in a model of a kennel. Well, Buttons

appears in the presence of the dogs with his great
bell, and the sensible brutes, conscious of the pain
they are about to endure, immediately set up a howl
of quadruple agony, to which the bell tolls its awful
accompaniment."

Exactly fifty years ago I went on a portrait-
painting tour into the country. Some sitters were
promised to me, and I had hope, subsequently
justified, that they would be the precursors of others.
Amongst my patrons was a clergyman of aristocratic
lineage ; who, though he had inherited little in the
shape of money, was possessed of certain tastes
common to the upper ten, in which he could not
afford to indulge ; but amongst them was the dinner-
bell, in which he did indulge, to the great annoyance
of his neighbours. The Vicarage was an unpre-
tending house with a small garden about it, in a
small village ; the inhabitants were chiefly Method-
ists, and the congregation at church was the smallest
I ever saw.

The Vicar was not popular ; the villagers dis-
liked what they called " his airs and graces,"
and they detested his dinner-bell. After sittings
from the Vicar, he and I took occasional walks
together, and one day, as we were passing a
cobbler's shop, the proprietor of it, " a detestable

little Radical Methodist," as the Vicar called him,
appeared at his door with a huge bell in his hand ;
he stepped into the middle of the road, and, affecting
not to see us, he rang it furiously.

" Man ! man !" cried the Vicar, " stop that ! What
are you making that dreadful noise for ?"

" Well, ye see," replied the cobbler, in the language of the county, " it's ma dinner-time, and aase
joust ringin' mysen in, to a bit of berry pudden."

I was so vividly reminded by the *Month's*
" Dinner-Bell Nuisance " of my early experience,
that I could not resist my inclination to introduce it
into what purports to be the life of John Leech,
in which it has no business whatever to appear.
Once more I apologize, and hope I may not be
tempted to " do it again."

Of all the Belles of the Month, the belle of the
month November is perhaps the most lovable.
There she stands on Brighton Pier—stands, that
is to say, as well as she can on those pretty feet of
hers, against a wind that is so boisterously rude to
her and to her mother, whose figure, blown out of
shape, makes a striking contrast to her daughter's.
The little dog declines to face the gale, which seems
likely to carry him away altogether, as well as the
struggling child behind.   The touches of cloud and

sea, together with the screaming gulls, are indicated
with the facile skill peculiar to Leech.

The Belle of the Month November "in Distress off a
Lee-shore—Brighton Pier."

In a paper headed " Hotels," Mr. Smith ex-
patiates somewhat tediously on the " old-established
house " of the " old coaching days." He says " the

inmates of the coffee-room were mostly commercial travellers." Those gentlemen may have been permitted to use the coffee-room ; but my recollection of such places tells me that the commercials always had a room of their own, specially provided for them.

The writer goes on to tell us that "the commercial gents," on the occasion of his discovery of them in the coffee-room, "pulled off their boots— not a very delicate performance—before everybody ; and then, after sitting over the fire, and drinking hot brown brandy and water until they were nearly at red heat, ordered 'a pan of coals,' and went to bed."

Yes ; and provided an excellent subject for Leech, worthy of being reproduced here, or anywhere, if only for that inimitable old chambermaid, who has lighted commercial gents to bed any time these forty years.

Judging from the twist of the commercial's necktie as he follows, or rather staggers, after the ancient maid, the brown brandy has done its work ; and it is ten to one against his carrying that box of patterns safely upstairs.

One boot is successfully removed from commercial number two, and it will evidently not be the fault of the man who is struggling with the other if it does not follow suit.

Let the observer note the marked difference in character in all these figures, as well as the skill and truth with which the details in the room are rendered.

In 1851 Bloomerism was in full bloom, or rather the attempts of few foolish people to make it prevail amongst us were so persistent as to bring upon them attacks by pen and pencil.

As I have already drawn attention to the craze, and to some examples of the way Leech dealt with it, I should have made no further allusion to the subject had I not found in the pages of the *Month* drawings of such charm that, in justice to the magazine and my readers, I felt I must notice them.

First, then, we have a Bloomer whip " tooling " her friends down to the races. If Bloomerism prevailed, this is the sight that Epsom might have seen in the year 1851, to say nothing of equestrian bloomers of whose horsewomanship Leech shows us examples.

I think in my last selection from the *Month* I might claim for myself a position resembling that of the pyrotechnic artist whose display of fireworks

culminates in a glorious blaze in the last scene of
his entertainment, if I were permitted to introduce it.

My firework takes the form of a bouquet of
young ladies at some "ancestral home" in the
country, who have just received a box of books
from London—perhaps from Mudie. What a bevy
of beauties!—two of them already absorbed in the
last new novel, while another makes off with an
armful of treasures.

When I say that this drawing—whether we regard
it as a composition of figures and of light and
shade, or as an example of Leech's supreme power
over grace of action and beauty—is worthy of admiration for itself, and of our gratitude to the
Month for the opportunity of reproducing it, I fear
no contradiction.

CHAPTER XII.

MR. ADAMS AND LEECH.

IN the pursuit of material for this memoir, I have had the good fortune to make the acquaintance of one of Leech's earliest and most constant friends, Mr. Charles F. Adams, of Barkway, Hertfordshire. This gentleman is the beau-idéal of a country squire — handsome, hale and hearty, though far past middle age.

The letters I am privileged to publish show the terms on which the friends lived, and prove beyond a doubt that many of the hunting scenes which sparkle so brilliantly and so frequently in the pages of " Life and Character " owe their origin to the opportunities afforded to the artist by his friend.

This long-continued intimacy commenced when the men were both young ; and the very first de-

velopment of Leech's taste for horses began with his
acquaintance with Mr. Adams.   It is told of that
gentleman that, being the possessor of two horses,
and being at that early time employed in business
in London during the day, the night served him and
Leech for a wild career, Adams driving his horses
tandem-fashion far into the country, rousing sleepy
toll-keepers and terrifying belated wayfarers, while
Leech's watchful eye noted incidents for future
illustration.

That Leech could sing, and sing well, I know, for
I have often heard him troll forth in a deep voice his
favourite song of " King Death "; but that he had
ever performed in public I was unaware till en-
lightened by Mr. Adams, who told me that it was a
favourite and not infrequent prank of these two
spirits to disguise themselves in imitation of street-
musicians, and, with the assistance of a young fellow
named Milburn, as wild as themselves, descend upon
the London streets, and by singing glees make "a
lot of money."

" Leech used to go round with the hat," said
Adams ; "but we never could make the fellow look
common enough.   Still, he collected a good deal,
though he failed on one occasion ; for, on presenting
his hat to a bystander, who had been an attentive

listener, the man claimed exemption as being in 'the profession,' in proof of which he produced a fiddle from behind him."

Barkway is in the heart of a hunting country, and the meets of the " Puckeridge " frequently took place near Mr. Adams' house, or at an easy distance from it. The house itself—a large mass of red brick, ivy, gables, and twisted chimneys—is one of those old places which have been enlarged to suit modern convenience without any sacrifice of the original design and quaint character.

"Ah," said my host, as he showed me into his dining-room, " what happy times we have had in this room, when Leech, Millais, Lemon—editor of *Punch*, you know, long ago—Tenniel, and others, found themselves round that table !"

The following letters, with their too few characteristic sketches, prove the affectionate intimacy between Leech and his friend.

"To Charles F. Adams, Esq.

" August 9, 1847.

" My dear Charley,

" You will be glad to hear that I have got a little daughter, and that both mother and child are doing well. Mrs. Leech was taken ill, unfortunately,

at the end of our trip to Liverpool—where, as
perhaps you are aware, Dickens and some of us had
been acting for Leigh Hunt's benefit—and she was
confined at the Victoria Hotel, Euston Square,
where she is now. I thought you would like to hear
the news, so send off these few lines. Give my
kindest regards to Mrs. Adams, and believe me,
old boy,

" Yours faithfully,

" JOHN LEECH."

In a letter written to Mr. Adams a week later,
Leech recommends a young gentleman to the care
of his friend, in the hope that if Mr. Adams has
" the opportunity, he will give the applicant something to do in his profession."   The letter closes by
this announcement :

"You will be glad to hear, I am sure, that
Mrs. Leech, *and my daughter !* are both 'going
on' famously.

" Ever, my dear Charley,

" Yours faithfully,

" JOHN LEECH.

"Given up hunting ?   Not a bit of it."

"January —, 1847.

" MY DEAR CHARLEY,

" Mark (Lemon) and I were talking only the other day about beating up your quarters towards the end of this month ; and, with your permission, if the frost goes, we intend to do so. We thought of riding down—I on the old mare ; and he on a ' seven-and-sixpenny.' . . .

" Is there anything in the shape of a good cob that could hunt if wanted down in your parts ? Possibly I could get rid of the mare in the way of a chop. I have been riding a nearly thoroughbred mare for the last week on trial. A very nice thing, but too much in this way.

" I want something more of this kind—a good one to go, and pleasant to ride.

" Yours ever faithfully,

" J. L."

"April 17, 1848.

" MY DEAR CHARLEY,

" . . . . Old Mark and I were special con-stables on Monday last. You would have laughed to see us on duty, trying the area gates, etc., Mark continually finding excuses for taking a small glass of ale or brandy and water. Policeman's duty is no joke. I had to patrol about from ten at night

till one in the morning, and heartily sick of it I was.
It was only my loyalty and extreme love of peace
and order that made me stand it. . . .

> " Ever yours faithfully,
>
> " JOHN LEECH."

My elderly readers will bear in mind April 10,
1848, and the monster petition of the Chartists,
which they were not allowed to present to Parliament in the threatening form they had arranged,
with other alarming signs of that troubled time—
the flight of Louis Philippe, Continental thrones
tottering, and the rest of it.

In his correspondence with Mr. Adams, Leech
constantly reminds his friend of his objection to
high-spirited horses. Under date February 18,
1849, he asks Mr. Adams if he can hire " an 'unter
from Ware."

" I should prefer," he adds, "something like the
old brown horse Mark had last year. If he comes,
of course he must have the same nag he had when
he was at Barkway ; *but, mind,* I won't have a beast
that pulls, or bolts, or any nonsense of the kind.
I come out for pleasure, and not to be worried.
Tell Mrs. Adams I shall not be half such an

objectionable visitor as I have been heretofore, seeing that I have left off SMOKING ! . . . .

" My very kind regards to Mrs. Adams, your little ones, and my good friends in your neighbourhood.

    " Believe me, old fellow,

                " Yours ever faithfully,

                        " JOHN LEECH."

                              " February 7, 1850.

" MY DEAR CHARLEY,

    " I am longing to see you, and have a ride across country with you. Do you think I could have the horse Mark Lemon had when he was down at Barkway ? Or if I couldn't have that one, do you know of any other that would be equally TEMPERATE and WELL-BEHAVED ? I have no horse at present. The last I had came down ; and I am rather particular in consequence.

" Give me a line, old fellow, and let me know when the hounds meet near you. . . .

                " Yours faithfully,

                        " JOHN LEECH."

One of Mr. Adams' daughters, Charlotte, surnamed Chatty —then a small child, now a lady whose age is borne so well as to make it difficult to believe that she lived so long ago as 1850—whose acquaintance I had the pleasure of making the other day, told me of her frequent visits to the Leeches, and of the never-ceasing care and tenderness of Leech.

In a letter from Broadstairs, written in the autumn of 1850 to Mr. Adams, Leech says :

" You will be glad to hear that Chatty is as well as possible, and is now going to have a long day's work (!) on the sands."

Again, after a good deal of horsy talk :

' Mrs. Leech and Chatty with her will return for good to Notting Hill on Saturday, when we shall be glad to have her with us as long as you can spare her. Apropos of dear Chatty, I am sure her mamma will be glad to hear that she has been uninterruptedly cheerful and well, and has certainly proved herself one of the best-tempered, best-hearted little creatures possible. She desires me to send you all her best love and kisses. . . .

" Ever faithfully,

" J. L."

" 31, Notting Hill Terrace,
    "February 18, 1852.

" MY DEAR CHARLEY,

" It will give me the greatest pleasure to come and see you. Mark (Lemon) says he will accompany me at the end of this month. Will that suit Mrs. Adams? I want much to SEE some hunting, as I want some materials for the work I am illustrating—indeed, I was going to propose a run down to you myself. Will you let us know when the hounds meet near you? Is the horse I had before still alive, I wonder? or could you, if I came, get me a horse 'in every way suitable for a timid, elderly gentleman'?

    *   *   *   *   *

" I was very glad to hear from you, old boy. In great haste, but with our united best regards to Mrs. Adams and yourself.

       " Believe me,

          " Ever yours faithfully,

              " JOHN LEECH.

" C. F. ADAMS, ESQ."

       " *Punch* Office, 85, Fleet Street,
          "Saturday, February 28, 1852.

" MY DEAR CHARLEY,

" 'The change in the administration' so upset our arrangements that I could not settle

what day to come down to you. I propose now
to come down to-morrow (Sunday) evening, so if
you can get me a rocking-horse, or a clothes-horse,
or any horse excessively quiet and accommodating,
I will go out with you on Monday. Mark, having
an appointment early on Monday with 'her Majesty,'
or somebody, will come on Tuesday, to hunt on
Wednesday, and back again on Thursday morning.
All this, of course, if it suits your convenience. At
any rate, I will come to-morrow, and then if there is
any difficulty, we can send up to town. With
kindest regards to Mrs. Adams,

" Believe me always,

" Yours faithfully,

" JOHN LEECH."

" 31, Notting Hill Terrace,
" Wednesday, March 17, 1852.

" MY DEAR CHARLEY,

" I had almost made up my mind to come
down on Friday evening to hunt on Saturday ; but
it would suit me infinitely better to come at the end
of the week following, as I am just now in the
agonies of my periodical work ; so let me know
when the meets are, and in the meantime I will peg
away and get my business done so as to have a
comfortable day with you. If I came on Friday, I

should have to work day and night before I went, and come back directly to work day and night again, which is not a pleasant state of things; I hope, therefore, that we shall be able to see the hounds next week.   I don't think Lemon would be able to come, as he is busy moving; but I will ask him.   I will make you the sketch of the house, or of anything else you like, when I come.

        " Believe me,

            " Ever yours faithfully,

                " JOHN LEECH.

" C. F. ADAMS, ESQ.

" Look in this week's *Punch* for a sketch on the Royston Hills."

            " 31, Notting Hill Terrace,

               " Wednesday, July 7, 1852.

" MY DEAR CHARLEY,

    " I congratulate both of you most heartily and cordially.   Mrs. Adams I hope is well, and will keep so, I trust.   I will take upon myself to say that I don't know any man more thoroughly capable of understanding and enjoying domestic happiness than yourself; and, moreover, I don't know any man who more thoroughly deserves to have it. You wish it had been a boy, do you?   Well, never mind; the son and heir will make his appearance in good time, I dare say. For my part, my unhappy experience makes me love little girls.

*   *   *   *   *

" Pray give my kindest regards to Mrs. Adams, and my love to Chatty, who is to kiss the baby for me, and

" Believe me, my dear Charley,

" Always yours faithfully,

" JOHN LEECH.

"C. F. ADAMS, ESQ."

" Barlow, Derbyshire,
"July 31, 1852.

" MY DEAR CHARLEY,

" You will see from the above address that I am still rusticating. I expect to be in rooms soon after the 12th of August, and then, after I have done my month's work, I am your man. You say where . . . Don't make yourself uncomfortable about the quantity of sport; I shall be quite satisfied with what you offer me. . . .

" Yours always faithfully,

" JOHN LEECH.

Here follows an admirable sketch of Mr. Adams waking up Leech with, " Now, Jack, my boy! There's no time to lose; we've ten miles to go to cover."

"Now Jack my boy! There's no time to lose We're ten miles to /0 to cover! —"

"Tuesday, December 14, 1852.

"My dear Charley Boy,

"Hip! hip! hurrah! The almanack is finished, and now for a day with the Puckeridge.

"I shall come down if you will take me in on Friday evening, to hunt on Saturday and Monday, I hope. Mark talked of coming. I wish he would. He says he should not ride, but that's all nonsense. Do you think Pattison has got a horse that would

carry him ? Oh, I have had a rare benefit of work !
I have been positively at it ever since I saw you.
I want freshening up, I assure you. . . . Lots of
fresh work, old fellow, so I think I may manage a
real horse soon.

  *   *   *   *   *

 " With kindest regards.

    " Ever faithfully yours,

       " JOHN LEECH."

       " Notting Hill Terrace,
        " January 26, 1853.

" MY DEAR CHARLEY,

  " If you could ride my horse to-morrow
(Thursday), pray do ; it would save your own, and
do her good. And the meet is close to you—
Langley Green. I should have written before, but
I have been harassed with work beyond measure.
And as it is, the first number of ' Handley Cross '
cannot come out until March. Mind you have the
mare well worked, there's a good fellow, as I don't
want, like our friend Briggs, to find her disagree-
ably fresh.

  *   *   *   *   *

 " Believe me always yours faithfully,

       " JOHN LEECH.

" C. F. ADAMS, ESQ."

"Saturday, February 26, 1853.

" My dear Charley,

" I suppose the frost has departed in the country, and that you have now what is called 'open weather.' It is very disagreeable here—wet, cold, and boisterous.

" However, if you can spare time (after riding your own, of course), I wish you would give the mare a benefit. I expect she will otherwise be a great deal too much for me.

*   *   *   *   *

" I am, my dear Charley,

" Yours faithfully,

" John Leech.

" C. F. Adams, Esq."

" 32, Brunswick Square,
'' Saturday, January 21, 1854.

" My dear Charley,

" Thank you for your note. I *can't* come down to-morrow, but I hope after next week to make up for lost time. I have got through some work that has been fidgeting me. I shall have a little more leisure. The meet on Monday is Dassett's, I see, so pray give it the mare; I have been so queer myself that I shall want her particularly 'tranquil.' I have sacrificed the moustaches for fear of frightening the horses in the field. They were getting too tremendous.

" *If, if* I can get away next week at all, depend upon it I will, for I want fresh air and a little horse exercise.

" With kindest regards, old fellow,

" Believe me always yours faithfully,

" JOHN LEECH.

" C. F. ADAMS, ESQ."

" Saturday, December 22, 1855.

" MY DEAR CHARLEY,

" How is the country ? I suppose no hunting as yet, for I have not received any card. The weather here to-day is mild and wet. I am working away in the hope of getting a day or two by-and-by comfortably. In the meantime, if there is anything going on, give my horse a turn across country, that's a good fellow.

" With kindest regards, believe me,

" Yours faithfully,

" J. L.

" If you can't spare time to hunt the mare, would it not be a good thing to send her to Patmore, and make him ride her ? But do you attend to her if you can manage it."

"8, St. Nicholas Cliff, Scarbro',
"August 30, 1858.

" MY DEAR CHARLEY,

" Your note was forwarded here, and I only found it on my return from Ireland, where I have been for the last three weeks. The consequence is that I am, of course, in rather a muddle with my work, and I am afraid I must forego the pleasure of shooting with you—at any rate, for the early part of the season ; so pray do not deprive other friends of sport on my account. I shall hope to have a day or two with you before the season is over. I am not a very greedy sportsman, you know, and as long as I get a good walk am pretty well satisfied. I am sorry you have been so unwell—you should really give yourself a holiday. The bow should be unstrung sometimes. I know I find it must. I wish you could have seen me catch a *salmon* in Ireland— a regular salmon ! When I say catch, I should say hook, rather, for he was too much for me, and after ten minutes' struggle he bolted with my tackle. It was really a tremendous sensation. . . .

" Believe me always,
" Yours faithfully,
" JOHN LEECH.

"C. F. ADAMS, ESQ."

" White Horse, Baldock,
                " Friday evening, ——, 1858.
" MY DEAR CHARLEY,

    *   *   *   *   *

" For the present I have arranged with Little
to make this place my headquarters, it is so handy
to the train, and I can come so much quicker and
later to Hitchin. The slow railway journeys take
it out of me, so that my pleasure is almost destroyed
by the fatigue of travelling and bother to get off. I
hope, nevertheless, that we shall have many evenings
together to talk over the *tremendous runs* that we
hope to have. I have bought a horse and brought
it down here. I hope you will be out to-morrow to
see it. I like it very much ; it is a most excellent
hackney, and sufficiently good-looking, although not
perfect, I suppose ; and it is represented to me as
being a temperate hunter in addition to his other
qualities. Well, we shall see. The black mare I
shall send to Tattersall's next week. She was as
fresh as could be last Saturday, and I was quite glad
I had not sold her ; but, alas! she was as lame in
the afternoon as possible, and next morning was a
pretty spectacle! She would not do at all. So much
for horseflesh.

          " With kindest regards,

                " Yours always,

                    " J. L."

" 32, Brunswick Square, W.C.,
" November 20, 1862.

" MY DEAR CHARLEY,

" If you *ever* have the time—which I never
have—I should feel so glad if you would go some
day and see how the 'party' at Kensington has
done his work.   I suppose 'that little form' of paying the bill must very soon be gone through, and I
should like to know from a competent authority that
the work has been well and properly done.

" How about the hunting?   I am continually
tormented here by noble sportsmen going by my
window in full fig.

" Yours always,

" J. L."

" 6, The Terrace, Kensington,
" November 27, 1862.

" MY DEAR CHARLEY,

" I am obliged to go to St. Leonards to-
night, but I should be very glad if you would to-
morrow, Friday (as you propose), look at my new
house.   In the corner of one of the new rooms I see
it looks a little damp, although they considered it
dry before they papered.   I must say I am pleased
with the new residence, and I think by degrees I
shall be able to make it pretty comfortable.   We
shall hardly get in here, I expect, much before

Christmas. There is yet so much to do. I shall
be very glad of any hints about improvements that
may occur to you.

"Kind regards, and believe me,

"Always yours,

"J. L."

There is amongst the pictures of "Life and
Character" a drawing of a sportsman who has been
thrown from his horse. He has fallen upon his
head, and as he raises it, stunned and bewildered,
and but half conscious, the sensations that must
have possessed him are realized for us in a manner
so marvellous, so wonderful in its originality and
truth, as to convince one that the accident must
have happened to the man who drew the picture ;
and this was the case, for the fallen man was Leech
himself, says Mr. Adams, who in charging a fence
was thrown, his horse falling at the same time. If I
had been told that the sensations inevitable under
the circumstances were required to be reproduced by
pencil and paper, I should have said such a feat was
beyond the reach of art ; but there they are ! As
the prostrate man looks up, he sees sparks of fire,
horse's head, legs, hoofs mingled together in a whirl
of confusion round his prostrate figure.

No doubt the work he undertook for *Bell's Life in London*, a long-established and long-discontinued paper, in which sport of all kinds was the most prominent feature—and which occupied much of Leech's time in his youthful days—contributed to the creation of a taste and love for field sports that always distinguished him. Quite a band of comic artists, including Cruikshank, Kenny Meadows, "Phiz," Seymour, and Leech, contributed sketches illustrative of a variety of subjects by a variety of authors; Leech's work being easily distinguishable from that of his brethren of the pencil.

CHAPTER XIII.

THE friendship, begun in their student-days at St. Bartholomew's, between Leech and Percival Leigh flourished in renewed strength by the discovery of similarity of taste—Leigh unable to draw, but possessing a truly humorous pen ; so the friends "laid their heads together," the result being the production of the " Comic Latin Grammar," letterpress by Leigh, illustrations by Leech. The first intention of the authors was that this should be a mere skit, a trifling brochure, consisting of a few pages; but, as so often happens, the work grew under their hands, and when published in 1840 it had assumed somewhat formidable proportions, and was followed by a work of similar character, with the title of " The Comic English Grammar."

The " Comic English Grammar " was a work full of pleasant humour, charmingly illustrated by Leech

" with upwards of fifty characteristic woodcuts." It
is curious to observe in these drawings the contrast
that they afford to the artist's later and more perfect
work. There is a timidity, and what we call a hardness, from which the sketches in " Pictures of Life

and Character" are entirely free; the general drawing, too, is faulty, but the humour and character are
all there.

The first illustration, given above, is from a ballad
called " Billy Taylor," popular in my young days, in
which Billy's true love—with the reluctance to part

from him common to persons suffering from that
passion—disguises herself as a man before the mast,
and shares the dangers of the sea with her sailor-lover:

"Ven as the Captain comed for to hear on't,
Wery much applauded vot she'd done."

The verb "applauded" has here no nominative
case, whereas it ought to have been governed by the
pronoun "he." "He very much applauded," etc.,
says the writer of the "Comic Grammar" for our
instruction. The second example, given above,

seems to me capital fooling, and an excellent proof
of the necessity for care in punctuation and accent

" Imagine," says the writer, " an actor commencing
Hamlet's famous soliloquy thus :

" ' To be or not to be ; that is.   The question,' etc.

Or saying, in the person of Duncan in ' Macbeth ' :

" ' This castle hath a pleasant seat, the air.'

Or, as the usurper himself, exclaiming :

" ' The devil damn thee black, thou cream-faced loon !
Where got's thou that goose ?   Look !' "

Here we have the fault of *hardness* that I speak
of, and something of feeble drawing, but the humour
is perfect.

After the publication of the " Comic Grammar,"
written by Gilbert à Beckett, one of the *Punch* staff,
a somewhat similar experiment upon the public
and on a larger scale was tried by the same author
in the issue of a " Comic History of England."
This venture was warmly opposed at its inception
by Jerrold, whose wrath at the idea of burlesquing
historical personages was expressed with vehemence.
Gilbert à Beckett persisted, however, and the history
appeared, with over three hundred illustrations on
wood and steel by John Leech.   The book is, as
might be expected, very light reading, containing

many puns and much play upon words. Leech's
work seems to me to be slight, hurried, and even
careless, compared with that of his later time ; but
the spirit of rollicking fun with which grave historical incidents are treated, and the humorous satire
that the principal personages receive at the hands of
the illustrator, make the "Comic History of England"
amusing enough. The following extract, with the
drawing that illustrates it, will show the truth of my
estimate of both.

"A story is told of a certain Fair Rosamond, and,
"though there is no doubt of its being a story from
"beginning to end, it is impossible to pass it over
"in English history. Henry, it was alleged, was
"enamoured of a certain Miss Clifford—if she can
"be called a certain Miss Clifford, when she was
"really a very doubtful character. She was the
"daughter of a baron on the banks of the Wye,
"when, without a why or a wherefore, the King took
"her away, and transplanted the Flower of Hereford,
"as she well deserved to be called, to the Bower of
"Woodstock. In this bower he constructed a laby-
"rinth something like the Maze at Rosherville, and
"as there was no man stationed on an elevation in the
"centre to direct the sovereign which way to go, nor
"exclaim, 'Right, if you please!' 'Straight on!'

" 'You're right now, sir !' ' Left !' ' Right again !' etc.,
" etc., his Majesty had adopted the plan of dragging
" one of Rosamond's reels of silk along with him when
" he left the spot, so that it formed a guide for him on
" his way back again. This tale of silk is indeed
" a most precious piece of entanglement, but it was
" perhaps necessary for the winding up of the story.
" While we cannot receive it as part of the thread of
" history, we accept it as a means of accounting
" for Eleanor's having got a clue to the retreat of
" Rosamond.

" The Queen, hearing of the silk, resolved naturally
" enough to unravel it. She accordingly started for
" Woodstock one afternoon, and, suspecting some-
" thing wrong, took a large bowl of poison in one
" hand and a stout dagger in the other. Having
" found Fair Rosamond, she held the poniard to the
" heart and the bowl to the lips of that unfortunate
" young person, who, it is said, preferred the black
" draught to the steel medicine."

Later on in the history we have another good
example of Leech's humour. King Edward, having
subdued the Welsh, " endeavoured to propitiate his
newly acquired subjects by becoming a resident in
the conquered country. His wife Eleanor gave
birth to a son in the castle of Caernarvon, and he

availed himself of the circumstance to introduce the
infant as a native production, giving him the title of
Prince of Wales, which has ever since been held by
the eldest son of the British sovereign."

QUEEN ELEANOR AND FAIR ROSAMOND.

A well-known historical scene is parodied as
follows : Henry IV. being ill, "the Prince of Wales
" was sitting up with him in the temporary capacity of

"nurse," says Mr. à Becket.   " The son, however,
" seemed rather to be waiting for his father's death

KING EDWARD INTRODUCING HIS SON AS PRINCE OF WALES TO
HIS NEWLY-ACQUIRED SUBJECTS.

" than hoping for the prolongation of his life ; and the
" King having gone off in a fit, the Prince, instead of
" calling for assistance or giving any aid himself,

"heartlessly took that opportunity to see how he
"should look in the crown, which always hung on
"a peg in the royal bedchamber. Young Henry was

UNSEEMLY CONDUCT OF HENRY, PRINCE OF WALES.

"figuring away before a cheval glass with the regal
"bauble on his head, and was exclaiming, 'Just the
"thing, upon my honour!' when the elder Henry,

"happening to recover, sat up in bed and saw the
"conduct of his offspring.

The Duke of Gloucester goes into Mourning for his
Little Nephews.

" ' Hallo !' cried the King, 'who gave you leave to
"put that on ?   I think you might have left it alone
"till I've done with it.' "

The savage and hypocritical character of Richard III. afforded Leech an opportunity for satire in his design of that monarch, when still Duke of Gloucester, in the shape of a crocodile shedding tears for the death of the two Princes in the Tower.

"Richard," says the chronicler, "by whom the "outward decencies of life were very scrupulously "observed, in order to make up for the inner de- "ficiencies of his mind, determined to go into mourn- "ing for the young Princes, and repaired to the same "*maison de deuil* which he had honoured with his "presence on a former occasion when requiring the "'trappings of woe' for himself and his retainers on "the death of his dear brother."

With the escape of Mary, Queen of Scots, I must close the extracts from the "Comic History of England."

"When the Queen was imprisoned at Lochleven, "a certain George Douglas," says the historian, "with "the sentimentality peculiar to seventeen, fell sheep- "ishly in love with the handsome Mary. She gave "some encouragement to the gawky youth, but rather "with a view of getting him to aid her in her escape "than out of any regard to the over-sensitive stripling. "Going to his brother's bedroom in the night, the boy "took the keys from the basket in which they were

" deposited, and, letting Mary out, he handed her to a
" skiff and took her for a row, without thinking of the
" row his conduct was leading to."

MARY'S ELOPEMENT.

A considerable interval of time elapsed between
the publication of à Beckett's " Comic English

Grammar" and the same writer's "Comic History
of England," the former being produced in 1840,
and the latter seven years afterwards ; but as there
is little or no appreciable difference between the two
works, either as regards the literary or artistic merit,
I have thought it well to introduce them in this
place.

These efforts show but one side of Leech's many-
sided power.   It was in " The Children of the
*M*obility," a satire on a production just then published, in which the children of the *n*obility were put
before the world in all the splendour of their aristocratic surroundings, that Leech's genius had full
play, the little Duke affording an instructive contrast
to the street arab, and the shivering, half-naked
beggar-girl becoming infinitely pathetic in her rags.
This work was executed in lithography, consisting of
seven prints ; and though, as works of art, they
bear no comparison to the wood-drawings of a later
time—they are not even so good as the " Fly-
Leaves " published at the *Punch* Office later on—
still, comparatively imperfectly as they are rendered,
they show the artist's intense sympathy with suffering childhood, as well as enjoyment in the games
and "larks " by which the sufferings are for a time
at least forgotten.

I now approach the period when the establishment of a comic newspaper was destined to afford Leech opportunities for the display of his powers, opportunities of which he availed himself with a prodigality almost as marvellous as the powers.

END OF VOL. I.

BILLING AND SONS, PRINTERS, GUILDFORD.
J. D. & Co.